DEATH
DOWN
EAST

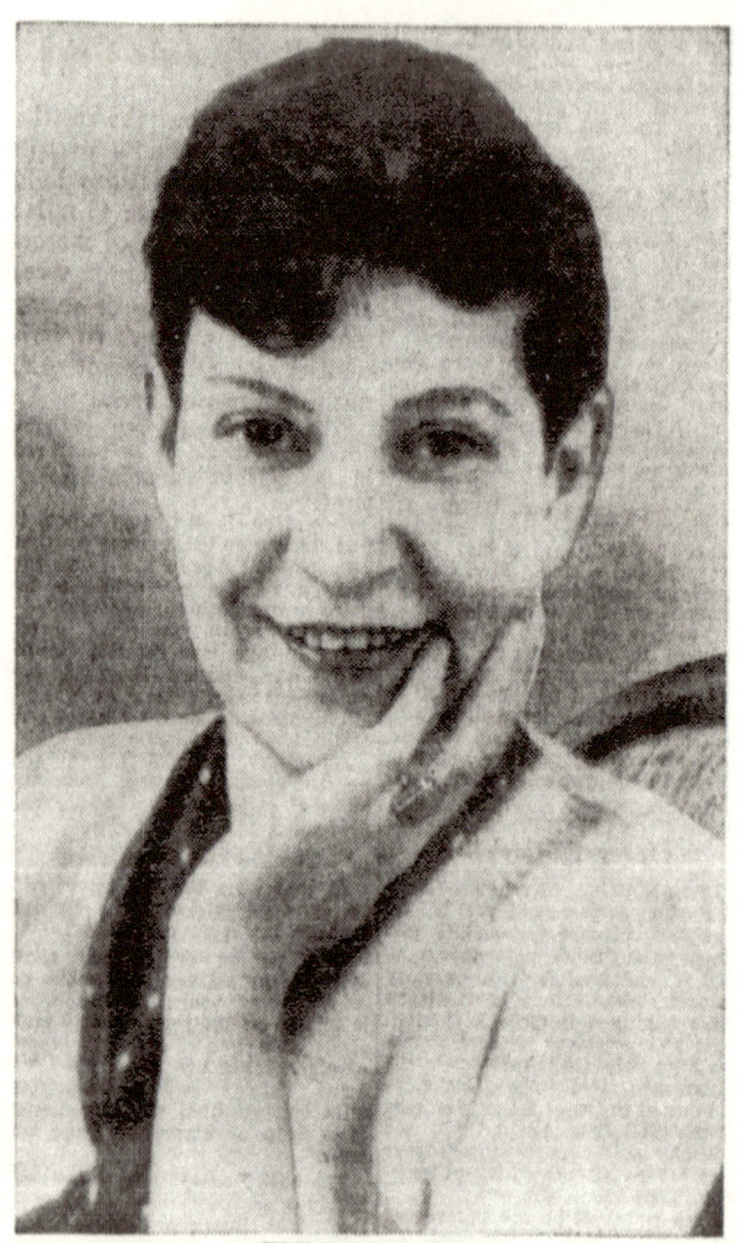

ELEANOR BLAKE

DEATH DOWN EAST

Eleanor Blake

COACHWHIP PUBLICATIONS
Greenville, Ohio

For My Mother

Death Down East, by Eleanor Blake
© 2022 Coachwhip Publications edition

First published 1940
Eleanor Blake, 1899-1952
CoachwhipBooks.com

ISBN 1-61646-538-7
ISBN-13 978-1-61646-538-4

1

It was pretty awful, sitting there in front of the fireplace and just waiting. Waiting while one person after another in a whole crowd of people you knew came up and asked if there wasn't anything you wanted and why weren't you dancing and wouldn't you like to go outdoors and get a little air. And wondering all the time which of them it was who was thinking that in a little while you would be dead.

I had to hold on tight and tell myself over and over that Mark Crosby knew what he was doing. That someplace among all the people who were milling around and jabbering with the radio turned up high so they could dance to it, Mark was listening and watching. And that when the right minute hit—the exact right minute—he would come in and save my life.

I tell you, it takes a simply amazing amount of faith in somebody else to put yourself in his hands like that and just say, "O. K. You tell me what to do and I'll do it." Particularly when you've had the ground knocked right out from under any faith you've ever had by realizing that of the people you have known since you were born—and considered a lot of them absolutely tops—there is one who is a murderer.

You see, none of us knew Mark Crosby until just before Alicia died. And of course a lot of them resented him. Especially the older ones, like the Herrods and the Willoughbys. An outsider coming in like that and sticking his nose into something at Sidley's Cove that everybody thought would be a lot better if it wasn't talked about. Then Mr. Richmond, of all people, asking him to stay on because he didn't really believe Alicia's death was as accidental as it seemed.

Mark is one of those tall men with a generous, warm mouth and eyes that look as though they know what you are thinking even before you do yourself. He has a long, rangy way of walking, and he stutters a little, sometimes, when he gets worried or excited. He's got a sense of humor, too, that doesn't always pick out the right people to be funny about, so you can see how he wouldn't go over with the Herrods.

He got along with the village, though, from the first, which is usually a lot harder, even, for an outsider to do than it is for them to get in with the summer people. Fred Mack, of course, which maybe wasn't so funny, seeing how things stood, but then Dr. Carver who's a good deal tougher.

I was pretty excited about him from the first time I laid eyes on him just because he was a detective, I suppose. And I thought everything he did was absolutely wonderful. Which is why he decided, I guess, that I could really help him some. That and the fact that I felt sorry for Alicia, too.

But I simply couldn't believe it when he told me that afternoon that I'd been picked on to die next. You don't, you know. And then I'd always been pretty unimportant as far as the Sidley's Cove crowd went—being the youngest and all that—so I couldn't see why on earth anybody would bother killing me. He had to shake me and tell me I wasn't going to walk out on him now—was I?—and stutter when he said it before the whole thing broke like a light and I realized that he was telling me the truth because he actually was scared stiff I'd be next. Anyway, he said I had to help him or he wouldn't be able to catch the person who had been doing it all.

"N-neatest t-trap of the w-w-week," he said, and that big mouth of his spread wide in the grin I like. But I didn't think it was very funny, specially since, what I was supposed to be in the trap was bait. I was pretty scared, but I hated to admit it, so I got cross.

"Don't be crazy," I said. "What would they bother with me for?"

He had got hold of himself by that time and wasn't stuttering any longer.

"Because they think you're smart," he said. "And you've been traveling around with me. If they finish me, the fun is over. But if they hurt me through killing you . . . You see, the whole thing's a swell illustration of one of my pet theories regarding crime: that crime, for the criminal, is a means to happiness through a sense of increasing power. If you're smart and I'm smart and they can hurt me through murdering you, they're a whole lot smarter, in their own eyes—and more powerful—than both of us together."

And besides, he told me, they thought I knew. If that isn't the silliest thing in the world. Me! I never know anything. Why the time Alicia died I just stood there looking down at her with all that blood and everything and I kept saying over and over, "She isn't dead, is she? She isn't dead?"

At least that's what Mark told me I said. For a long time I couldn't remember. Because it was after that that the other things happened and everybody began to change from thinking it was just an awfully bad luck year at Sidley's Cove to going around in a state of absolute jitters.

So you can see how it all piled up and why I was pretty shaky that afternoon and had just about made up my mind

I wouldn't go to the Festival at all when Mark said come on, we'd drive over to the ocean side and watch the surf come in and talk things over. I didn't have any particular mad passion to walk along the beach where we had had the clambake the night Alicia died, but I'd come to the point where I'd do anything Mark asked me to, so of course I went.

Being late August you couldn't count on the weather, and the wind was blowing east, coming in mean and nasty from the water, and I shivered with cold and I suppose fright, too; and Mark took off his leather jacket and put it on me.

That's one of the things a lot of people didn't like about him—the way he dressed, I mean. He just went around most of the time in a brown suede coat and gray slacks and a white shirt open at the throat. He said he had to dress in town and that was enough for any man. What made it all the worse, of course, is that he looked about ten times as well as anybody else in the crowd, being so big and easy in the way he moved.

When he'd put the jacket on me he stuck his hands in his pockets and began walking along the beach so fast I had to double time to keep up with him. And then he told me.

After I'd got over being scared and was simply mad I asked him why on earth should I stick my neck out? Did he have to go and get dramatic just because he was a detective, and spring traps and everything?

I could see by the way his mouth looked, just moving without any sound, that he was trying to hang onto himself and get the words all shaped before he let any of them out. He didn't quite, though, because he stopped and glared down at me and said,

"D-don't be a l-little f-f-fool!" And he took hold of the fronts of the leather jacket and his hands, thin and strong and big-knuckled, were right under my chin and he shook me until my teeth clicked. That made him feel better, I guess, because he sailed right in.

"I didn't lay any trap. I just found one, understand? It's another dear soul that's been laying traps all along, and I've just stumbled onto it in the usual dumb fashion that's given me such a brilliant reputation in my trade. Found it before it was too late. Because this time it's set for you. Get that? Get it through your funny little head?"

I stood there, digging the crazy, wooden sole of one of my sabots into the sand and turning absolutely white, I guess. The surf was pounding in, making an awful racket and he said something and I said, "What?" and he simply roared:

"I CAN'T PROVE IT!" and then he said, "Let's clear out of this," and took hold of my arm and hurried me along back to the car. "I can't prove it unless I catch 'em at it. Slick as oysters. I'd look pretty, wouldn't I, marching up to any of that smooth crowd and telling 'em they'd committed two and a half murders this summer and were getting ready to commit another and not a spit of evidence to prove it? No sir! Let 'em lay their trap. Let 'em think they're going to catch you in it the way they've caught the others. Th-then I'll c-catch *th-th-them!*"

I guess maybe if he had just kept on talking the way he usually did I wouldn't have been able to believe him. Not quite, anyway. But I'd got so I knew that whenever he stuttered it was because he was excited and being terribly honest, and I absolutely adored him for it. So I just looked at him and said:

"O. K. You tell me what to do and I'll do it."

"Thank God!" he said, and the way his nice wise dark eyes went all warm with relief made my heart come right up in my throat. "First thing—you're not to back out of the Festival. Do you hear?" Naturally, I didn't say a word.

"O. K. Now listen, when you get dressed go straight to the Willoughby's and sit down in that big chair near the fireplace in their living room. The one with the doo-hinkies— what do you call 'em . . . ?"

"Wings," I said.

"I guess it's wings. Anyway, the one that faces the door. You sit down in that chair and don't you get out of it until you see me in the doorway giving you the high sign. When I do you say yes to whoever has asked you to do whatever it is—no matter how harmless or unimportant or frightening it seems. Hear? Until that happens I don't care what you do just so you keep on saying no. Tell 'em you've got a whale of a headache only you're just too noble to go home . . . or act mad or bored or any of that female stuff you want to pull. Only don't look scared! And *don't stir!* Not until you see me standing in the doorway and nodding yes in no uncertain terms. Then get up and go along and know that I'll be keeping you in sight even if you can't see me. They're going to try to finish you tonight and I'm going to catch 'em at it. Before they have time to do it. Understand?"

I said yes, but I wasn't feeling any too good about it and I suppose he must have heard the shaky way my voice acted because he put his arm around me while we drove home, and I just let go and dropped my head against him and had a good cry.

We pulled up in front of the house and I saw Leslie and Arch Herrod and Gerry Hunter and Tess and the two Willoughby girls and my mother working like crazy to get the booths done in time, and Tess yelled at me and I waved back and said all right, I'd be there, and I got out of the car and Mark said:

"It's all over but the shouting, Kathie. Just sit tight. Unless I miss my guess—and I won't—we'll have it in the bag by midnight. It'll be nasty, but there won't be any more accidental deaths at Sidley's Cove."

I suppose I nodded, but anyway I walked across the lawn toward the others and I heard him put the Fiat into gear and he drove off. And that's the last I saw of him until long after the Festival had started and I'd been sitting in the big wing chair in front of the Willoughby's fireplace for simply ages, scared stiff and trying not to show it and looking up at the door to see if Mark was standing there every time anybody spoke to me.

It really was pretty awful, sitting there wondering when he'd show up and knowing that among all those people I'd known since I was born, practically, was one who meant to kill me. And wondering how. Thinking, as I had thought so much that summer, about those who had died and trying to remember all about it. But all I could remember, in the silly mouse-in-a-maze state my mind had got itself into, was that every single time there had been a death the wind blew east.

I tried to get it out of my head and make myself remember something else, but I saw the little, licking flames in the fireplace flicker the way they always did when there was a cross draft into the chimney because it hadn't been built right, and I smelled the sweet, heavy odor of wood smoke that came out in a quick, gray puff. Mrs. Herrod's voice boomed out, "There's an inshore wind!" and I shivered and my hands grew damp and cold with fright and I sat there with my teeth clicked tight together just saying, "Mark . . . Mark . . . Mark . . ." over and over down in my throat. And it seemed to me that the only important thing in the world was for me to remember so that I would know what it was going to be before it had time to happen.

2

Alicia was the last person in the world you would ever think anybody would want to kill. That is, if you didn't know Sidley's Cove.

She was rather slender and tall with simply enormous eyes and she did her straight, soft brown hair in two braids that she wound around her head in a crown. And while her tennis wasn't very good and she was pretty ordinary at swimming, almost any man in the crowds would rather dance with her than have a drink, which is certainly more than you could say for any of the rest of us. Even Tess. There was a kind of flavor, too, about the way she talked. Not brains exactly, but a special charm that made her stand out in a crowd.

She was under a terrible handicap when she first came up, because Mr. Willoughby started out by calling the Richmonds outsiders even before he had seen them. Not that anybody blamed him then. The Sidley's Cove crowd isn't what you would call wealthy and it certainly isn't society; it's just got the habit of sticking together and usually looks at anybody new the way a Persian tabby looks at an alley cat that's wandered into the yard. They don't intend to be mean. I know, because I've been one of them since before I was born. But they're just so darned busy with one thing and another from the time the season opens in late

June until the Festival closes it with a bang before Labor Day that they don't get around to being nice to strangers. And then, the Richmonds coming in the way they did . . .

It was the last week in June, so it hadn't really warmed up yet, but somebody—I think it was Tess Conover—had tried the water around two o'clock and said that for her part she was going in. Of course the rest of us had just been waiting for somebody to do that and anyway we wouldn't be stumped so we'd gone in and come out again pretty fast and were lying around on the sand which was nice and hot, and Ruth Willoughby said she guessed she would go and see if the mail had come in yet.

She came back along the beach from the store running, her bright terry robe flying out behind her, and the thick cork of her shoes kicking up the sand. Almost anything was news in the middle of the week like that, so when she sat down we were mad at her for being out of breath and making us wait.

"It isn't so much," she said. "It's just the old Greene place is taken."

Tess was feeling pretty contrary because Gerry Hunter had written her that he couldn't get up from town that week end, and, being engaged to him, she naturally felt that without Gerry, she'd have a mighty slow time at the dance. So she sat up and began looking around for a cigarette and said:

"What do you mean, it isn't so much? Who's taking it?"

"Some people named Richmond."

"That's a lot to know. What else?"

"They're from New York."

"New York," Tess said acidly, "is a very large city."

"Well, I can't help it!" Ruth is the mild kind. She's always had a pretty good disposition, but she gets rattled when anybody starts riding her and never knows what to

say. So most people think she's being sulky when she's
really trying not to pry.

"Oh, for goodness' sake, Tess, let her alone," I said. If
there was anything I didn't see any sense in getting started, it was a row over some new people in the Greene place.

But Tess had got her teeth into a good battle and didn't
intend to let go. Tess is like that.

"Well, don't you want to know?" she said. "If anybody
really in-teresting is taking the Greene place . . ."

It might have been the way she said interesting that
made Helen Willoughby mad but maybe it was because she
was getting tired of the way Tess was everlastingly riding
her sister, Ruth. Helen isn't the mild kind at all and she's
got a keen brain, too, and a sharp tongue when she wants
to use it.

"The only thing you ever mean by in-teresting," she
said, "is: 'Is there a man in the crowd?'"

It was all getting pretty nasty and I didn't see why on
earth it should and I was trying to think up some silly
kind of thing to throw in to bring it back into line when I
saw that Tess had done one of those quick changes of hers.
She had rolled over on her elbows on the sand and was
looking up at Ruth and smiling.

"The trouble with Ruth is that it's upset her no end
about the Greene place. She's afraid that when she and
Arch get married they'll have to spend their summers with
Arch's folks instead of having a house of their own. Fess
up, Ruth!" She laughed and Ruth looked kind of sheepish
and laughed, too. "Not that I blame you," Tess said.

"Oh, the Herrods aren't so bad," Ruth said.

"Yes they are. Specially Mrs. Herrod. She bosses everybody. Except Arch. He can stand up to his mother a lot better than Les can. And a whole lot better than Mr. Herrod.
There's somebody who's hag-ridden if anybody ever was."

"S-s-sh . . ." Ruth said and she gave a quick, nervous little look over her shoulder. "She might hear."

Tess laughed "Do her good. Everybody's simply got the habit of kowtowing to her. Come on now, Ruth. Give! That's a darling. You can't tell me you just went down to the store and somebody—who was it, Bill Hennebery?—told you the Greene place was taken and you turned right around quick and started running back here without finding out another single thing."

"I *told* you what I found out. Their name's Richmond and they're from New York and they're moving in this week. And it wasn't Bill that told me. It was Fred Mack."

"Fred? How's he know?"

"They've hired him to work for them. Mr. Richmond has."

"Good heavens! How can he? Fred's practically the Herrods' family retainer. Will that raise a row! Mr. Herrod'll . . ."

"Part time," Ruth said.

"Worse and worse. Sidley's Cove divided against itself."

"Oh, Tess," Helen cut in, "you're making a mountain out of a molehill. Fred really hasn't enough to do to keep him busy on the Herrods' place all the time, and he might just as well make some extra money if he can. You know very well there's no work up here in winter—or next to none—and if Fred doesn't pick up all he can during the season he practically starves by spring. The Herrods won't mind. They're awfully reasonable. Really . . ."

Tess's eyes got that funny look they always get when she's going to spring something.

"Have these Richmonds," she said, "got a boat?"

Ruth was fussed all right. "I don't know. Fred didn't say. I tell you, I didn't just stand there and stand there in the store and ask a lot of questions about something that wasn't any of my business. Fred told me and I said wasn't that interesting and he said they were coming up this week and I left."

"Because," Tess said slowly, turning over on her back and shading her eyes from the sky that was an awfully hot, bright blue, "if I'm any good at putting two and two together, they have got a boat. If they didn't have a boat they couldn't have finagled Fred into working for them—part time or any. *And* if they do have a boat Fred will work for them for practically nothing. And if they have a boat and Fred tries to divide his boat time between them and the Herrods, Mrs. Herrod just isn't going to be reasonable at all. No sir! Not—at—all! If they step on her toes she's going to call these Richmonds from New York outsiders and simply *fre-e-eze* them out of Sidley's Cove."

It sounds rather nasty and of course I suppose it is, but I don't know what anybody can do about it really. If your grandfather and some of his friends are people who found a spot up north that they liked a lot even before you were born and built summer places, and all your folks have grown up knowing each other and the people in the village, you just get to feeling it does belong to you and anybody you haven't asked in yourself has no business being there. Which made it hard for the new people who began to come in after the war when some of the families couldn't keep their places up any more and others died out.

That's what happened to the Greene place. Tommy Greene died, and the Greenes kept coming up but anybody could see their hearts weren't in it and then last year they put their house on the market—Mr. Greene's in real estate in town. Nobody blamed them, really, but we all felt a lot better when it was just a young couple that took it the year before, and they minded their own business and only on summer lease at that. And then this year when it was

empty again everybody knew that Arch Herrod and Ruth
Willoughby were going to try leasing it for next season
after they got married in the fall.

Ruth said if these Richmonds were only leasing it, she
didn't see why it should affect her plans, but Tess wouldn't
let it go at that.

"How do you know they're only leasing it? The Greenes
would a whole lot rather sell it than try to keep it up for
renters, and you certainly don't know that the Richmonds
haven't bought it. Do you, Ruth?"

"For goodness' sake, why can't you let me alone?" Ruth
had found a flat pebble and she stood up and was trying to
skip it. I suppose it made her feel all the more helpless that
she missed. Because when it just hit the water with a plunk
she began looking around for another one with a kind of
concentrated fury that wasn't like her at all. It's funny how
things like that can seem important and maybe it didn't
to anybody else but me. I only know I was terribly relieved
when she picked up a nice thin one and it skipped three
times, just as pretty, and she sat down and said in a milder
voice that sounded a whole lot more like herself, "And you
don't know, Tess, that they've got a boat. Do you?"

"No. But I bet I'm right." Tess laughed, and her laugh
could smooth your feathers when she wanted it to as easily
as it could ruffle them when she felt like being annoying.
She always knew just when a barb had gone deep enough
so that it was ready for real trouble in another minute and
she had an uncanny way of suddenly giving it two points
and turning one of them on herself to fix things up. "And I
won't let the Greene place business alone, Ruth, until I've
found out whether there's a man in the crowd," she said,
and everybody laughed with her and felt better.

A little outboard somebody had across the bay cut out
from shore and began running around in circles and we
all watched it, lying there just soaking in the sun and not

saying much. Mr. Herrod hated outboards so that he nearly had apoplexy every time one showed up. He said he could see no excuse for anybody's deliberately making such an offensive noise on a quiet body of water. The whole bunch of us were crazy about them, of course, and Arch was simply dying to build himself a little racing shell and put one on but he couldn't make his father budge an inch.

Well, we got tired looking at the outboard after a while and our side of the bay beach faces east and the afternoon sun had dropped behind the trees in back of us and a little cold wind had sprang up, and Ruth wrapped her robe around her and got up and said she was going in to dress, and was anybody else coming? Just then the up train whistled in and Tess said, sure, and that for her part she was going down after the mail and get Fred Mack in a corner and find something out. So it ended by our all going to the store together.

It's funny how you do things in a summer place that you wouldn't be caught dead doing at home. We were all old enough by now so that whatever men there were in the crowd were working in town and didn't get up except for week ends. Only the older ones, sometimes, like Mr. Willoughby and Mr. Herrod and, of course, Arch. But then Arch didn't really count because he was engaged to Ruth, and anyway we were all so used to his dabbling around with paint that we didn't even get very excited when he had a one-man show the winter before in town. That was just Arch Herrod. So we girls danced together a lot, trying out all the new records as fast as they came out. You can see it was kind of hard on the men when they did come up because we were usually way ahead of them and ran them ragged on the new dances that all they knew about was what they'd seen in the rotos.

Fred Mack wasn't around when we got down to the store and of course you couldn't get to Bill Hennebery till he was done with the mail, so we put nickels in the Carola and danced in the pavilion while we waited for the mail to get sorted and the little ground glass window behind the wicket to be pushed up.

The pavilion is built out over the water and you can see the bay through the windows on three sides, so Tess must have been looking a lot closer than the rest of us or maybe it just happened. Anyway, she stopped dancing all of a sudden.

"I bet I win my bet!" She snapped her fingers. "Look there!" She pointed out the end windows at a boat that was cutting the water with its nose up, and throwing out two white wings on either side as it headed for the dock.

Well, we all stood absolutely stock still because of course we knew every boat on the bay and while outside boats do sometimes run in, it looked a lot as though Tess was right this time. The boat came straight ahead with that exciting kind of roar you only get in really good ones that have been built for speed; and then it throttled down as nice and easy as you please and simply glided alongside the pilings, and we saw Fred Mack at the wheel having the time of his life.

Fred was nearly sixty but he had been practically born on the water, what with his folks being fishermen just about ever since Sidley's Cove began way back in history someplace. He stuck it out fishing, too, and I don't suppose he would ever have gone in for caretaking for a resorter if Mr. Herrod hadn't bought the *Felicity* six years ago. Once Fred got his hands on that motor he was lost. And here he was now, playing with a new one. We knew right away, of course, that the new one must belong to these Richmonds, and that there was going to be trouble all right.

The window behind the wicket in the post office went up with the little bang Bill Hennebery always gave it so we would hear it out in the pavilion and we looked at each other as though it was the most terrible thing in the world that the mail was out, because we were simply dying to go and ask Fred what was what. And then Tess said, "Thunder with the mail!" and ran through the store and around onto the dock and we followed her like a lot of ninnies, stumbling and falling over each other. Tess called out,

"Fred! What do you mean, working for a bunch of outsiders?"

I remember the way Fred's nice, old leathery face looked then just as plain as day. Of course it was always sort of Indian color and never bleached out, even in winter. I know because I saw him the February we came up after our kitchen wing burned. But when Tess said that—and so loud I know you could hear it clear inside the store—he turned red through all that tan, and we thought he was ashamed. He was, too, but not for himself.

He just got out of the boat and jumped up on the dock and began tying her up and didn't say a word and we crowded around him and Tess said, "Oh! Look! It's called the *Lark*. I can't stand people who pun their boats."

And then Alicia Richmond came up out of the forward cabin and just stood there, looking at us, and there wasn't any color in her face at all and her eyes were like the eyes of a little girl when she's scared to death of a lot of grown people and isn't sure what they mean.

3

The crazy thing about hurting somebody else is that you want to avoid them like the plague afterwards. I'm no psychologist, goodness knows, so I don't know why, but I do know it's so. Or anyway, that it was so about all of us and Alicia Richmond.

We felt like such absolute fools. None of us ever having laid eyes on her in our lives before and having struck out and simply hit her before she had a chance.

Tess was the first one to get hold of herself, of course. We all stood there like a bunch of dumb statues. Honestly! Just as though we had been turned to stone. I must have looked even sillier than the rest because I know my mouth stayed open for, anyway, half a minute. And then I saw Tess shrug and turn away and say, "Mail's out!" and start walking across the dock toward the store with that little, swinging arrogant saunter of hers. I hated her then. I really did.

Which wasn't fair of me because it was Tess who broke the ice and went out of her way to try to make it up to Alicia for the way we had treated her when she first came up. You see, Tess isn't really mean at all, though I suppose the way I've talked about her, it sounds as though she was. It's just that she's more nervy than the rest of us. Mr. Herrod once said that when he was younger a girl like that would have been called fast, but he supposed things were different these days.

I think that, really, he liked her, the way we all did. You couldn't help it. Because if she took digs they were always straight digs. And if she thought anything she would come clean out with it instead of nursing a grudge or talking about you behind your back. She wasn't an ounce afraid of what anybody else thought and would do what she wanted to do and what she felt was right in the face of the devil himself.

None of us said a word about what had happened on the dock all the way home. We talked about the mail we'd had that day as though it was the most important thing in the world. I remember that what I'd drawn was a catalogue from one of the sports shops and all the way up I kept looking through it and simply screaming about the marvelous clothes I could get if I were in town. Me! I'd stocked myself up to the neck before I'd left. It was just that I was self-conscious and ashamed and so were the rest of us for a while.

But Tess had had a letter from Gerry Hunter, and after she had finished reading it she tucked it in the pocket of her cardigan and looked at me and grinned. "Gerry says he loves me," she said, and she looked so little girl and vulnerable all of a sudden, I could have hugged her. She started whistling, then, and tramped along the road with that strong, proud swing of hers that could look so darned snooty sometimes. She was right beside me and all at once she stopped whistling and said,

"She's not bad-looking."

"Who?" I said, and then I woke up. "Oh! You mean the Richmond girl! No, she looks pretty nice to me."

"Tell you what—" Tess slipped her arm through mine— "if she's got a brother you can have him."

It's that sort of thing that made some of the others mad. But I liked it. It was Tess. Ruth always said it sounded as though Tess thought she could have anything she wanted and had decided to be big-hearted instead. But it wasn't really. It was just the way Tess gave the signals for the game.

We didn't see much of the Richmonds for a week of two after that and Fred Mack and the Herrods did have some kind of a row, but Fred could talk an engine into starting when nobody else could even budge it, and he must have smoothed things out some way or other because there wasn't much what you'd really call thunder. Not nearly as much as we expected. Even the Willoughbys seemed to take it pretty well because Helen said her folks harangued about it just one night downstairs after she'd gone to bed and she heard her father stay it didn't matter to him as long as that man minded his own business and her mother said that she supposed it was his own business after all and her father gave a sort of a nasty laugh and said, "What— scavenging?"

I remember thinking when we found out what Mr. Richmond did and that he was Richmond's Soap, that you have to make soap out of . . . well, whatever it is you do make soap out of . . . don't you? And I didn't see that it was any worse than pharmaceuticals which is what the Willoughbys do. So that went on, and then it died down after awhile.

It was the Wednesday before the dance we cooked up to celebrate the Fourth of July long week end that Tess stepped out and made friends with Alicia, only she was still just the Richmond girl to us then, of course. The water had warmed up a lot and we had all been in, climbing around on the float and diving and all that. From out there we could see the Greene place, as we all kept right on calling it even after the Richmonds moved in; and along about three o'clock the tall girl we had seen on the boat that day came out of the house and walked down across the sand. Maybe it was because she was so tall and slender and had such pale, transparent skin—but she looked lonelier to me right then than almost anybody I'd ever seen. She was carrying a book and had sun glasses on and she dropped the book and her robe on the beach and slipped out of her sandals and went across to the water and waded in. You could see by the way she did it that she hadn't done much swimming, and when she finally got in she moved around pretty close to shore with a bad crawl stroke that Helen Willoughby said set her teeth on edge.

Tess just sat there on the raft swinging her legs in the water for a while and all of a sudden she slid off and started to swim for shore.

"Where you going?" I yelled at her, but she just looked back over her shoulder and made a mouth at me and smiled.

"Cigarette," Helen said. "She can't live twenty minutes without one."

I climbed up and dived, and when I came out of the water and was back on the raft again I looked to shore and saw Tess walking along the beach toward the Richmond girl. I kept watching them both, simply fascinated, because while I'd been fussing around with the idea of doing something about her I hadn't; and the chances are it would have taken me half the summer, and then I'd have muffed it. And if you think either one of the Willoughby girls would ever have pulled themselves together to go and tell somebody new like that that they were ashamed of themselves for being rude, and wouldn't she like to come to the dance—well, you just should have seen their faces when they realized what Tess was up to. Ruth looked positively scared. But then, she often does.

I stood it as long as I could and then I took off and headed for shore to back Tess up. The two Willoughbys must have held a conference or something and decided they couldn't hold out alone. Anyway, they followed me a minute or two later and we must have looked pretty silly kicking the sand up with our toes as we strung along the beach.

Tess and the Richmond girl were sitting down by this time and Tess had managed to cadge one of her cigarettes, and was looking pretty pleased with herself. "I've said, 'Sorry, please,' for all of us. Just explained we were brought up right but it didn't take. Her name's Alicia." Tess nodded to us one at a time.

"Alicia Richmond—Katherine Edwards—Kitty for short.

"Helen Willoughby—the blond one.

"Ruth Willoughby. Helen and Ruth. You can't do anything much else with those names. I'm always Tess—Tess Conover—except when I can't help it—like putting down Letitia for a passport or something terribly legal like that."

We all began jabbering at once to help hide the fact that we were embarrassed, and before I knew it I was really interested. She was rather amazing-looking and she talked in a quiet, suppressed-excitement sort of way. Tess told her we were doing a dance over the Fourth and we'd like her to come.

"And if you've got a man up your sleeve," Tess said, coming right out with it, "you'd better bring him along. A brother, I mean, or anything like that. We run low on men around here."

Alicia shook her head. "No," she said. "Only my father. Unless Mark Crosby comes on up." She frowned and a funny, strained sad look came into her eyes. "Mother's dead, you know."

"I'm sorry," Tess said and then she smiled. "But that makes us even. There isn't any father in my house and my mother's awfully good-looking and amusing. Men always like her a lot. I hope your father measures up."

The strange cloudiness was still in Alicia's eyes, and it seemed to me she was having a hard time smiling. "I hope he does," she said.

"Who's Mark Crosby?" I thought maybe it was a good thing to get her mind off whatever was bothering her, and anyway I wanted to know.

"He's . . . he wrote *I Shot the Albatross.*"

"Oh!" I said. I could see it didn't mean anything to any of the others, but I'd read it and had been terribly excited about it. It was one of those books that had made quite a lot of noise the winter before on the non-fiction list—all about criminal investigation and that sort of thing.

"Do you think he will come up?" I said. "I mean Mr. Crosby. I'd be thrilled to death to meet an honest-to-goodness detective like that."

But Alicia was looking past me, over my shoulder and not paying attention to anything I'd said. I glanced back and saw it was only Arch Herrod and told her so.

"Arch is our permanent male. He paints."

"Yes, I know." Alicia's voice was very soft. "I saw his show in town last winter. It was—it was pretty fine."

It must have been the tone she said it in—rather breathless somehow—that made me turn and simply stare at her. Of course we knew that Arch was good—we had to unless we thought the critics were absolutely balmy—but you see we had all grown up together and were used to thinking about Arch as the Herrod boy who had a temper and mooned around. All except Ruth Willoughby who had managed to get herself engaged to him. Tess and I never could figure how.

You had to admit that Arch was good-looking. Big and tawny with a perfect mane of hair growing thick and rather wild and an easy way of walking that had a lot of grace to it. He came ambling along the beach toward us, his long legs and his heavy, muscular chest and shoulders a nice warm bronze in contrast with the blue of his swimming trunks. It was all there, you see, only Arch didn't ever do much about it. Even with Ruth he was pretty absent-minded and would forget a date about half the time because he'd get wrapped up in his work.

Tess called to him, "Arch! Come here and be introduced."

He waved at us and stopped and picked up something on the beach and stood nursing it in his hands, just looking at it. Ruth said,

"Oh, heavens! He's probably got a shell."

He still had it when he came up to us and he held it out. It lay pink and fluted in the dark palm of his hand, and Alicia took a deep breath and said, "Yes," and he looked up at her.

She had taken her bathing cap off and her brown hair lay in that crown of braids around her head and her dark eyes were terribly large in her white face.

"Oh, my God . . ." Arch said.

There was a perfectly awful silence for a minute only Arch didn't notice it at all. He just kept on looking at her and Tess broke it by saying, "Alicia Richmond—Arch Herrod," and then, "Let's go in again while it's still warm."

She ran across the beach and into the water with a lot of splashing, and Helen and I followed her. When I reached the raft I saw that Alicia and Arch were still standing there on shore, just looking at each other. And that Ruth was looking, too.

4

You know how a storm builds. The weather is sunny and clear for quite a while—just going along day after day so that you take it pretty much for granted. And then one morning you wake up and everything feels close and sticky and you're restless and you don't quite know why. The sun shines through a haze, all coppery and hot, and little tight electric currents run through your nerves, tying them in knots. You snap at anybody who says the least thing to you and you keep watching the sky that has slowly darkened into a great, blue-purple back drop. And you're afraid that a simply terrible storm is going to break. And you're afraid it isn't.

You see, the trouble was, that it wasn't only Arch who made such a fuss over Alicia Richmond. It was Gerry Hunter, too. And Les and even Mr. Herrod, looking, with the puffy bags under his eyes and his heavy jowls, like a silly old Newfoundland trying to be young again. In fact it was just about everybody except Mark Crosby. I remember thinking that if my own folks hadn't always been so crazy about each other they didn't know there was anybody else in the world, Dad would have fallen for her too. But I know now, of course, that it wasn't Alicia's fault.

It didn't make much difference to me because there wasn't a man for me anyway—at least there wasn't at first, and I was kind of used to playing tennis with the little kids most week ends or running around on a boat with Fred Mack whenever he'd take me or even wandering into the store half the time when there was a dance and talking to Bill Hennebery. You get that way when you're the youngest one in a crowd, and everybody else is paired up.

But all the others got mad about it. Even Tess. And she could usually call on that swell sense of humor of hers to pull her through. You see, it was made up of such little things. Like the way Gerry acted on the Fourth.

He had come up on the night train instead of driving, so he'd be there Saturday morning and have the whole week end. We all went down to meet him, along with Tess, the way we always did. Except Alicia, who had been terribly decent after we talked to her on Wednesday and hadn't pushed herself at all. Gerry got off the train and put his arm around Tess and kissed her in that nice, casual, easy way that made you feel they had something so sure and strong they didn't have to show it off.

Les Herrod was on the train, too—he and Gerry both work in Cummings Greene's office in town—and when they got off there was Mark Crosby. He'd introduced himself to Les and Gerry on the trip up and they'd got talking. Les was kind of stiff about it, but Gerry was all right, and of course we were tickled to death to have another man in the crowd, and I was excited because Mark was the man who had written *I Shot the Albatross*.

Gerry had had one of his grand, silly ideas and had brought us up a whole bunch of harmonicas to fool with, and we were playing at them, making the most horrible screeching noises as we faced along the bay road. And then I saw Alicia. She was walking with her father, slowly, in the shade of the trees, and the thin beige linen of her dress blew a little in the wind. It was perfectly plain with a low, square neck that made her throat seem terribly white. We stopped to let Mark Crosby out, and Alicia looked up and smiled at us.

"My God!" Gerry said, and turned around to stare after her, as we drove on, in a perfectly gauche, little-boy way. "It's Alicia Richmond!"

"For heavens' sake!" Tess said, "Do you know her? How come?"

Leslie Herrod always had been dead pan, even his voice. But it sounded flatter than ever as he said, "We both knew her. Gerry and I. In school."

"Oh, co-ed! Well, she'll be at the dance tonight."

"What a pair of eyes . . ." And that's all Gerry said.

Maybe, as Tess said afterwards, Alicia didn't have to use her eyes all the time, but I still think she couldn't help it. They were that kind of eyes. Anyway, it seemed to be all over but the shouting for Gerry. It wasn't that he was nasty to Tess; it's just that he concentrated on Alicia—hard. He hung on every word she said that night and danced with her every dance he could get. Which, between Arch and Mr. Herrod, wasn't very many. And Tess couldn't laugh it off.

Ruth didn't even try to laugh it off when, a day or two later, she waited an hour for Arch to keep a tennis date with her and then started hunting for him. We all tagged along, the way we usually did, calling Arch's name like a bunch of kids. Tess was on ahead, turning it into "Archie" just to make him mad, and, when she came out of the woods at the side of the Greene place, she stopped dead still. Ruth was beside me and I'll never forget the look on her face when she saw.

Not that Arch was doing anything you could really kick about. It's just that in the little birch grove on the lawn in front of the Greene place Alicia was sitting in a big white wicker chair, and the sun and shadow of the birch leaves made a moving pattern on the pale blue of her dress. And

Arch, with his back to us, had his canvas up and was paint-ing in a sort of fever so that he hadn't even heard us call.

Mr. Richmond came out of the house and walked across the grass toward us, and, honestly, we didn't know what to do. He'd been perfectly grand at the dance and every-body had liked him a lot. He was big and good-looking, and he and Mrs. Conover had got along simply fine from the start, so that she had gone to town for the Richmonds when the Willoughbys began talking about them pretty acidly the next day. And there he was, waving at us, very friendly, and for the second time since we'd met Alicia, we felt like fools.

"It isn't her fault, Ruth," I whispered. But Ruth just stood there with the same funny, frustrated look on her face that she had had the day she picked up the pebble and tried to skip it, and she turned around and walked back along the path through the woods alone without saying a word.

As for Mrs. Herrod, she never laughed anyway, of course, but the night her dignified, important, middle-aged James made a fool of himself over Alicia, she absolutely froze.

You see, part of the trouble was that there wasn't a thing anybody could do about it. We'd taken the Rich-monds in about ten times faster than we ever took in any-body new simply because we had been so rude to Alicia the first time we saw her. And there we were—with about half the men apparently ga-ga over her and Mark, being a guest of theirs, pretty popular with the young crowd, specially me, and then Mrs. Conover and, her father . . . Anyway, you can see how we couldn't drop them, even if we'd had the nerve. So they got asked to everything. Even the bridge the Herrods played every night with the terrible regularity of a clock.

The bunch of us usually shied away from the bridge tables and, if we couldn't stir up something down at the pavilion, took it out in ping-pong at the Herrods' house or the Willoughbys' or bowled with duck pins in the alley my dad had put up in our basement. We soon found out, though, that Alicia didn't go in for sports.

"I'd love to," she said, the first time we asked her to play ping-pong with us. "It's just that I'm so terribly bad." And she looked at us with those sad, enormous eyes. "I'd only spoil your game. Go on along—please. Just don't mind me . . ."

But she didn't play bridge, either. She'd sit in a big chair over in a quiet corner, and sooner or later one of the men—Arch, who had decided he didn't want to play, either, or Mr. Herrod, or even my father if he was dummy that hand—would get up and go over to see if there wasn't something she wanted.

Which is what happened the night Mrs. Herrod practically insulted her to her face. We'd all been sitting on the beach—Ruth and Helen, that is, and Tess—singing and looking out across the bay to where a little, young moon was rising. After a while Ruth said she was cold and was going in. It was pretty obvious that what she really wanted was to keep her unhappy, restless eyes on Arch, but we said all right anyway and went up the path under the pines to the Herrods' house.

When we trailed in, Mr. Herrod was bending over Alicia's chair, and as I walked past I heard Alicia say, "No, really, Mr. Herrod, I hardly ever sing any more." She smiled up at him and laughed in a little self-conscious flurry the way people do when they want to be teased. He was holding a match for her cigarette with the silliest, most gallant gesture in the world. ". . . except once in a long time just for Papa. Papa!" she said, "Please tell Mr. Herrod I'd rather not sing."

Mr. Richmond was up to his ears in bridge with Mrs. Conover for a partner and having a perfectly swell time but when she said that he looked up, rather startled, I thought.

"What?" he said. "What's that?"

Alicia's voice held a fine, faint note of sharpness.

"Won't you please tell Mr. Herrod that I honestly don't want to sing?"

"Oh! Certainly, my dear. I can understand . . ."

He looked terribly confused and I saw Mrs. Herrod simply glare at Mr. Herrod's back, and she stood up, pushing her chair away from the table so abruptly that she nearly tipped it over.

"James!" she said in the deep, dictatorial voice she used when she ordered her gardens or organized entertainments or any of that sort of thing. "Will you sit in, please? Mary prepared refreshments before she left tonight. I'll bring them in. Personally," she turned deliberately and looked at Alicia, "I'd rather not hear Miss Richmond sing myself."

So you can see how things were by the time we had the clambake the third week end in August. Everybody was there. Even Mark Crosby. So I was pretty keyed up and I think Tess and Ruth figured that a clambake would put them one up on Alicia at the start. She was like a hothouse flower that flourished only indoors or in a calm, sheltered place, and Tess had high-pressured everybody into having this picnic on the ocean side.

"It's plenty warm," she said, "for tackling surf. And anyway, there's a lot more driftwood over there. We can have an honest-to-goodness fire for a change."

So we packed up in three cars, taking Fred Mack along to help with carting things and because he knew more about that shore and a lot more about doing clams, really, than any of the summer people.

"Of course Fred's going," Tess said. "Get him in front of a driftwood fire and give him a drink or two and he can think up stories to amuse the folks. It'll keep 'em from tearing home for bridge the minute the sun goes down, and we can get in one more swim before we have to leave."

When we started out, I remember, the wind was from the west, and Tess was terribly disappointed because she was afraid there wouldn't be much surf. There wasn't either, but we found a lot of driftwood that was nice and dry from the last big storm. I was still pretty shy of Mark, but he was being awfully nice to me, and I was so excited and happy I didn't know what I was doing.

Of course the clams were about half sand the way they usually are, but everybody expected that, and we had plenty of sandwiches and salad and hot coffee, and somebody—Mr. Richmond, I think it was—had been angel enough to bring along a whole lot of hamburgers, all made up, and two grills for us to do them on over the coals.

We were cold, too, by the time we got out of the water, and about an hour after we had finished eating the wind turned and began to blow east. The sun had set and the moon hadn't risen yet so the whole shore line was dark except for the light the fire shed. You could hear the surf beginning to pile in and just make out the long white froth of the breakers. Alicia, who had only dabbled her toes in the water a little that afternoon when it was still calm, was down shore a ways, standing looking out over the ocean, all alone. And suddenly, lifting her head, she began to sing.

"Oh, you'll take the high road and I'll take the low road . . ." her voice was blown back to us, so beautiful it made you catch your breath, and the fire flickering, lighting the great, jagged rock behind her and her beach robe flying in the wind. The song ended and her voice died out, leaving a silence, and then everybody began jabbering at once, as though they couldn't stand it.

Arch said, "She ought to come back here to the fire. She'll catch cold."

But Gerry was already on his feet. "I'll take her my coat."

I guess the whole thing was too much for Tess. And Gerry's doing that, the last straw. "Don't be silly," she said. "What's so special about her?"

She jumped up, pulling Ruth with her and grabbing Arch's hand as she ran. And she called out in a high, hysterical voice that didn't sound like hers at all,

"Alicia Richmond, you're going in!"

Alicia had just snapped her lighter, and, when she turned as though she had been spun round like a top, the east wind fanned the flame so that, before it was blown out, I saw her white face and her huge, terrified eyes.

For a long time that's all I could remember. Even when Mark told me that I screamed, "She's afraid! She's afraid!" and started running toward her, I couldn't make my mind bring it back to me.

But that night when I sat there in the Willoughbys' living room with all those people I knew milling around me and wondering where on earth Mark had got himself to, and the beat of the music in my ears from the swing band that was on the air and Mrs. Herrod's voice quite near me saying, "There's an inshore wind . . ." it came back to me, sharp and clear, like a picture with sound.

I remembered that those same people had been crowded around me when I stood there with the wind piling the breakers in over the jagged rock where Alicia had fallen. And while the water swirled around her white, bruised face, washing the blood away, I just kept saying, over and over:

"She isn't *dead*, is she? She isn't *dead?*"

5

There's a game we used to play when we were kids that was called, "Red Light." The person who was "It" stood with his face to a wall and his eyes covered with his hands, just to make sure he couldn't see. And you ran and tried to hide while he counted fifty. When he came to fifty he said, "No moving, no talking, no hiding—red light!" and took his hands away and opened his eyes and turned around, and if you hadn't managed to hide yet you had to stand stock-still, whatever position you were in. Because if you moved even the tiniest little bit or made a single sound, you had to be "It" instead. And then everybody else moved, too.

I remember that that crazy game came into my head when I heard my own voice that night Alicia died. Because before that it was just as if everybody had been turned to stone, standing there with their shadows falling across Alicia onto the rock and when I spoke it was as though I'd broken a spell and everybody could be themselves again.

That is, if you want to call it being yourself to start giggling the way Ruth Willoughby did. Of course everybody knew it was simply hysteria because she began to cry right away afterwards, but it was pretty awful to hear somebody laughing like that, just the same.

Ruth was nearest Alicia, too, having been on the end of the line that Tess Conover had made when she took her hand and Arch's. When Ruth started laughing I looked at her fast, and all I could think of was her face when she'd managed to make that pebble skip that day. Close and tight, still, and sullen but with something triumphant and "I'll show you" about it, too. And then she began to cry and her father put his arm around her and led her back across the beach to the fire.

It wasn't until then that I noticed Mr. Richmond was standing right beside me. I saw the rosy end of the big cigar he was always smoking shaking in his hand against the dark. It must have taken him a minute or so, too, to realize what had happened, because it was only then that he tossed the cigar into the water and went down on his knees in the wet sand beside Alicia.

"J-just a minute, th-th-there!" Mark Crosby called out, and his dark, strong hands were on Mr. Richmond's, holding them back. He said something to him fast, very low so I couldn't hear what it was, and Mr. Richmond stood up and everybody began crowding around him in the stupid, self-conscious way people do when something's happened and they're not sure what.

I suppose I knew even then that things were worse, really, than they seemed, because I stopped looking at anybody else and just watched Mark. The water was washing down and around and over Alicia's body, and I thought how terrible it was not to lift her out of that right away and I saw Mark's sure fingers find her pulse. He dropped his head down on her breast, listening, where it showed so white above the pale blue of her swimming suit, and, when he looked up and while he was trying to say it, I was in a perfect agony for him because he was excited and couldn't get the words out.

"G-g-glass! Looking g-glass! Have any of you g-g-girls g-g-g . . ."

He stuck on that line like a broken record and looked around at us desperately and all of a sudden it dawned on me and I started running back toward the fire where I'd left my purse.

I had the little mirror out of it and ready for him by the time I got back, and he held it close up against Alicia's mouth, reaching in his pocket with his other hand for the brassy-looking foreign lighter he always carried. He spun the wheel and the wick caught and flared up and he looked at the mirror and slowly shook his head.

"We'd better get her home," he said in a heavy voice to Mr. Richmond. "No use . . . not moving her . . . and the tide . . ."

Mr. Richmond just stood there for a minute as though he hadn't heard. When the words came out at last it was as though there were lead weights on them and they had to be dragged. "She's . . . dead . . . too . . ." he said, and there wasn't even a question in his voice.

"Yes," Mark said. I saw him look quick at Mr. Richmond and he bent over and slipped one arm under Alicia's shoulders and the other under her knees, and he carried her, her beach robe streaming, to the Richmonds' car.

A lot of us had come over in it, piled on top of each other, some of us, laughing and talking as we drove, because the Herrods' car was filled with stuff for the picnic and just Ruth and Helen had come with their father and mother in the Willoughbys', though goodness knows why, because it's a seven-passenger that they always drive up in from town; and Mark's Fiat was only a roadster without even a rumble seat. But naturally we couldn't crowd into the Richmonds' again because of Alicia and everybody knew that Mr. Richmond wanted to get her home as fast as he could. And of course Mr. Richmond was just about out on his feet and needed somebody to go back with him. It's funny how you can manage to be happy at a time like that; but when I saw Mark Crosby looking around and knew that what he was looking for was me, my heart jumped right up in my throat for pure, crazy joy.

"You go on with Mr. Richmond," I said. "I'll drive your car back. I . . . I'd love to," and thought to myself, You crazy fool, are you going to start stuttering now, too?

"Good kid!" He gave me a quick little pat on my shoulder, and I kept feeling his hand like a blessing for a long time afterwards, and I kept thinking, Isn't it grand? He likes me.

I suppose Arch Herrod hadn't quite got his nerve up yet or maybe he was only brooding on just how to say it in the slow, concentrated way he had; but he didn't make a sound until Mark stepped on the starter of the Richmonds' car and shifted into gear. All I know is that his big, blond head suddenly loomed up in the spread of the car's lights. Of course a light like that always does throw deep shadows but I knew it wasn't only that that made his face look so perfectly ghastly,—and his eyes like empty sockets in his head.

"I'll go along," he said to Mark. "There ought to be somebody . . . in back . . . to hold her." And he opened the door and stepped inside, and as the car pulled away I saw him bending over Alicia as he held her in his arms.

Maybe you don't think it's a dreadful job—getting every-thing picked up and everybody together after a beach party when something like that has happened. If it hadn't been for Mrs. Herrod, I don't suppose we ever would have got organized. Or anyway, not for hours.

You see, for one thing, nobody wanted to talk about it and yet they did. It was the only thing on anybody's mind, of course, but it was so mixed up with all the other things they were thinking about, too, that they couldn't say a word without making a mess of things.

Like when Gerry Hunter began picking up knives and forks and utensils to take home. We'd all brought our own silver, and everybody'd brought a pan or two, and he had some crazy idea, I guess, that he could keep them straight. Anyway, he called out in the hushed voice we'd all taken to using.

"Who do these belong to?"

I looked up and saw that he was holding the two big iron grills and I said:

"The Richmonds," and right away I felt as though I'd committed some sort of dreadful crime that nobody'd ever forgive me for.

A minute or two later Helen Willoughby, who had stood up under it all a lot better than Ruth, said:

"Here's a purse. Who . . . ?"

It was Alicia's—the little one she carried with her make-up in it and all that. I said so and I managed to get out that I'd give it to Mark and then I couldn't go on, and Mrs. Herrod positively roared in that great commanding voice of hers:

"Come now. There's no use everybody's going to pieces! We've some work to do here and we'd better all make up our minds we're going to do it and get it over with. There are three hampers. Put everything in them just as you find it. We can sort out afterwards at home. Gerry, you pick up the heavy things and Helen can fold the blankets. Ruth . . . where's Ruth?"

Mr. Willoughby said, "Ruth's over there. With her mother. She's . . . she seems to be in a bad way. Shivering and all that. I've got her wrapped in a blanket and I've tried to get her to wait in the car until we're ready to go, but she . . . she doesn't want to be alone."

"All right," Mrs. Herrod said briskly. "But that doesn't prevent Leslie's giving Fred Mack a hand there with that hamper. And Kitty . . ." She had that eagle eye of hers on me by that time and she sniffed.

"You driving that young man's car back?" I suppose I must have said yes, or nodded or something because she went on wrapping up the sandwiches that had been left over. "Very well! Then you might as well burn up the trash and wait until we're all through and put the fire out before you leave. Nothing's going to hurt you. And bring Tess Conover when you come. Her mother can go with us and she's wandered off down shore." She sniffed again. "Just when she's needed," she said, and began putting paper covers on the salt and pepper shakers, screwing them down tight inside the tops.

If I hadn't known Mrs. Herrod so well I suppose I would have thought she was being pretty horrible, but ever since I was a youngster I'd been used to having her take charge like that and order people around and generally run things, and even though I'd never liked her, I figured it was just her way. It seemed so natural to all of us that nobody thought it was funny she could keep right on doing it even after the dreadful way Alicia had died.

All I know is that it seemed simply ages to me before they stopped that fussing and piled into the two cars and I heard Mrs. Herrod say, "James! What on earth's the matter with you? If you're going to clash the gears like that, it's high time you let somebody else drive," and the cars ground from first into second and then to high and headed off into the night, leaving me with only the light from the fire that had died down to coals.

I'd been all right until then. I suppose because there'd been a lot of us together and we had kept busy and I hadn't realized what had happened and how it was bound to affect us all. Not really, that is. But when everybody was gone and the cars had driven away, the night seemed to close in on me and the ocean was big and huge and impersonal, pounding in with a steady roar, and I remembered that I was supposed to find Tess and bring her home with me and I started calling her name as loud as I could.

But the wind whipped the words out of my mouth and carried them inland, away from the shore, and nobody answered and I looked up and down the beach, but I couldn't see anything because the fire had died down so low and I was in a regular panic and ran over and turned on the lights of the Fiat and blared the horn and yelled, "Tess! Tess! Tess!" over and over at the top of my lungs.

When I saw her, finally, walking toward me with that vigorous stride of hers, her hands in the pockets of her beach robe, I was so glad I nearly cried.

"For heaven's sake!" I said. "What on earth did you have to scare me like that for?"

There was a funny smile on her face that I didn't like, and I didn't like the look in her eyes, either. She just stood there for a minute and then she said:

"Don't be an ass, Kitty. I wasn't giving you a second thought. I was thinking about my own sweet neck and wondering how it would look in a noose."

"Tess!" I said, and I felt goose flesh standing up on my arms.

"Oh, don't 'Tess' me!" It was all there—all the directness and courage and strength that was Tess, but the way she said it made me feel as though she'd slapped my face. "You don't think, do you, that they're going to let me off without giving me the works?

"It was me who yelled at her, wasn't it? And me who ran toward her so she was scared half out of her wits? It was me who made her turn like that so the wind took her robe and wrapped it around her tight. She took one step and it tripped her and she fell!"

"Tess," I said, "Tess, come on home. Come on, Tess, get in the car."

Tess opened the door and slid in and I climbed under the wheel. I stepped on the starter and shifted and she said:

"And if it's motive they're looking for, it's all there. Sure, I wanted her out of the way. Sure, I hated her. Only it doesn't seem to me that if I'd consulted myself about it beforehand I would have figured I could get Gerry back by killing her."

6

I didn't say a word all the way home. I couldn't. I just sat with my hands on the wheel and my foot steady on the accelerator of the Fiat, that I'd thought would be so much fun to drive, and kept my eyes on the road ahead. It was a narrow, gravel, country road that wound in and out among trees and shrubs that had grown close and low, making green archways over the car. The leaves picked up the light and reflected it so that I saw Tess's hands, pressed tight on each other in her lap.

I couldn't say anything because I didn't know what Tess was thinking, and I wasn't even sure what she had meant. I was afraid to tell her that she couldn't be blamed for an accident dike that—not really, because I wasn't sure she thought it was an accident. And what with her saying that and being so terribly bitter and ironic about it and so defiant and brave and scared my thoughts went scrambling after each other in a crazy circle until I ended up by not being sure it had been an accident, after all.

Which was a nice spot to find myself in just as we came to the path that led back from the bay shore road to the Conover's house and I had to stop and let Tess out. But I had to say something. Tess was my best friend. I couldn't let her go like that.

"Tess," I said, "Tess!" I caught one of her hands and held it. "It doesn't matter what happened. I'm back of you to the last ditch. You know that, don't you?" She had that funny little smile on her face, and I couldn't stand it, so I said wildly, without thinking much about it, but just because I thought maybe it would make her feel better. "Mark Crosby is, too. I know Mark'll help you if there's any trouble . . ."

She squeezed my hand and dropped it and her eyes looked scornful and wise and lost.

"Oh, no he won't. What do you think he's up here for?" And she turned and walked away from me along the path.

I kept thinking about that while I drove on to the Greene place, so I didn't notice at first that Dr. Carver's car was parked on the road in front of it and that all the lights were on in the Richmonds' living room. I didn't notice much of anything, I guess, until I'd stopped and started to get out and heard Mark stuttering right beside me.

"Wh-wh-what the hell t-took you so d-d-d . . ."

"Damned long!" I always get cross when things don't make sense and I'm being pulled every-which-way by a bunch of feelings. "You don't think I was just dawdling, do you? For the fun of it?"

Mark laughed. "Keep your temper, Kathie. Nobody wants it. I was getting worried about you—that's all."

"Here's your car," I said, "safe and sound. And if you want to blame somebody, blame Mrs. Herrod . . . or Tess."

The next second I was mad at myself for saying that, because of course he pounced on it like a cat on a mouse.

"What have they been up to?" He'd snapped his lighter for my cigarette, and I could see his eyes, dark and watchful, fixed steady on me.

"Oh, for heaven's sake! Is everybody going to start going around being suspicious of everybody else? Because if they are . . ."

"If the shoe fits," he said, "wear it. If it doesn't, stop making such a row and tell me what happened."

I'd been getting pretty hysterical, I guess, and that brought me up short.

"Mrs. Herrod," I said, "went around organizing everybody. You know the way she does. Made us all pitch in and help clean up. And Helen found Alicia's purse and I was going to bring it to you, and then Mrs. Herrod began ordering us all around and I didn't see it again."

"Alicia's purse?"

"Yes, the one she carried to the beach with her—with her make-up in it and all that."

"Who had it last?" Mark said, and I thought he was just being stupid and then he said, "Helen Willoughby? Lord, yes! Go on."

"I really can't blame Mrs. Herrod, though. Because of course Ruth wasn't good for anything, and Tess had disappeared."

"Disappeared? What do you mean? Vanished?" He snapped his fingers. "Pouff! Just like that?"

"No. If you'd wait . . ."

"O. K."

"Anyway, Mrs. Herrod got everybody lined up so we got things together, and everybody packed in the two cars and she told me to put the fire out and bring Tess along with me when I came. And they left and I couldn't find Tess. I mean," I said in a hurry, "not right away. She was off down the beach someplace by herself and I called and called and finally she came and . . ." I stopped. I couldn't help it. I was remembering the way Tess had looked and what she said.

"And she was all broken up over it, wasn't she?" Mark said. "Not over Alicia's death, of course, but over the fact that she might be blamed for it. Ironic and all that?"

"Yes." I know I must have sounded pretty defiant. "And why wouldn't she be?"

"Why, indeed?"

"If I'd done what she did . . ."

"Only you wouldn't." He was leaning against the trunk of a big oak, watching me, and he looked so satisfied with himself and cocksure and safe, I almost hated him. I blurted out:

"If I'd been in her shoes . . . if I'd loved Gerry and been engaged to him and Alicia had come along and Gerry had gone goofy about her that way, I . . . I'm not at all sure I wouldn't have wanted to kill her, too!"

I could have bitten my tongue out the second after. It's the last thing in the world I'd ever meant to tell anybody. What Tess had said, I mean, when she was still so terribly upset and scared and everything. I was simply furious at myself. And at him.

He put his hand on my arm and just looked at me, and I began batting my eyelashes so I wouldn't cry.

"Remember this, Kathie," he said, "if you ever find yourself on the stand: Keep your temper. Rule number one in good, sound legal strategy is to make your witness angry."

He took a fresh handkerchief out of his pocket and snapped it open and dabbed my eyes with it in the clumsy, useless way men do and said, in an easy, matter-of-fact voice,

"You haven't really told me anything, you know. A person can't be hanged for thinking. Though if Tess told you she really wanted to kill Alicia, the information could be used for making trouble if it fell into the wrong hands. If you'd spilled it, for instance, to somebody who had a good reason for making it his business to take it to Art Stewart. Stewart would probably jump at it like a dog at a throat. Being new in office as a prosecutor, all Stewart wants along about now is a death by violence and a motive that will hold water so he can put on a show for his constituents. He wouldn't even care if the case was thrown out of court for lack of evidence. There'd be a bunch of voters in the grandstand who would spread it around that he had gone to town for the people versus, and that's all that really matters when you're new on a job."

I'd stopped crying by that time and I gave him back his handkerchief.

"Come on, now," he said. "The more I know the less I'll have to blunder around in the dark. And the less I blunder the better things will be for everybody. Don't answer until you've thought it all out and you're sure you're telling it right. Did Tess say, in so many words, that she ever wanted to kill Alicia?"

I didn't have to think. "No," I said, and I told him what Tess actually did say and how I'd gone around in circles about it, trying to figure out what she meant.

"Yes," he said slowly, "it does show a certain degree of malice."

He looked back over his shoulder at the house where you could hear men's voices coming through the open door.

"Dr. Carver's about ready to leave," he said, and then, "The point is that if there's an investigation—if we can't manage to convince Stewart and the sheriff that it was an accident so they get their noses off the trail—it's likely to be bad for Tess. That is, if she was thinking about how she'd like Alicia to be dead when she called out to her like that and ran down to the shore. Because if she was—and admits it . . ." He tried to smile, but it was a pretty feeble attempt.

I thought about Tess and what a swell person she was and how terrible it was that Alicia had come to Sidley's Cove. "What'll happen?" I said.

"Stewart could bring it in as manslaughter probably—without half trying. Whether he could prove it or not is something else."

All I could say was, "Oh no! Oh no . . . !" and look up at Mark as though if he tried he could keep it from happening.

"Listen, Kathie. You'd better tell me all about it. Exactly what she said and how she acted. Confession is good for the soul—and it's damned good catharsis, too—as Tess has probably discovered by now. If you spill it to me you won't be in much danger of telling bits of it to anybody else. And I'll keep it all bottled up inside me. Honest, I will."

So I told him. Every bit of it. But when I came to the end where I'd let her out of the car and I'd told her I was back of her and Mark was, too, and that he'd help her and I remembered how she'd looked at me and what she'd said, then I stopped dead.

"Go on," Mark said, "Give."

I shook my head.

"O. K. You don't have to, because I know. She said I wouldn't help her and what did you think I was up here for. Right?"

I was feeling pretty stubborn, I guess and it must have shown in the way I nodded, because he laughed.

"Well, she's wrong," he said. "Because it so happens that it fits in with my plans just fine to help Tess Conover right now. With some good, sound advice, anyway. You'll be seeing her tomorrow, won't you?"

"Of course."

"O. K. Then tell her for me that if Brownlow and Stewart get her in a corner and begin to ask her questions— which they will if I don't succeed in stopping 'em before they start—she's to stick to facts. That's all they have a right to, as things stand now. She can tell 'em what happened—to the best of her knowledge—but she doesn't have to go turning her soul inside out and show 'em the lining. If she feels there's something else she absolutely must get off her chest she'd better tell you about it or—whether she thinks so or not—me. As a father confessor I'm tops. I don't report to anybody but myself."

I heard Dr. Carver saying "Good night," and I saw Mr. Richmond's big body outlined in the open doorway and then Dr. Carver's quick, plump little figure, with the thick bag he always carried swinging briskly in his hand, come toward us over the sloping lawn.

Mark's voice was very low and he said fast, "Listen—what do you know about Gerry Hunter?"

"Not much."

"No more does anyone else. Except Leslie Herrod, perhaps, and I'd rather not talk to him. Look here—Hunter and Les have to take the down train in the morning for town. Can you make it your business to drive them to the station and pick off how Hunter's taking this whole thing? Impression only—if that's all you can get. However, if you can make him talk, I won't mind."

In the light from the lamps of the car, I could see that Mark was smiling. That made me mad.

"What on earth *are* you up here for?" I said.

Dr. Carver stopped and said, "Hello, Kitty—how's your mother?" and then, "Crosby, I'd like to see you a minute."

Mark said, "Certainly, doctor. Kathie, you get in the car and wait. I'll run you home."

But I only shook my head and started walking down the road toward our house. There was a lump in my throat, and I was lost and bewildered and I didn't know who to trust any more because I was absolutely sure that even if Dr. Carver hadn't come along just then, Mark wouldn't have told me.

7

From the Greene place to ours isn't very far and I'd walked it so many times it seemed to me I knew every bit of gravel on the road that ran along the bay between them. First there's Herrods', with a lilac hedge separating the two houses and a lot of great, gloomy pines towering in front of it and shutting the sun out, even on bright days. The Willoughbys' comes next, a big rambling frame with a lot of gingerbread scrollwork trimming the porches and the gable ends, and after that the Conovers'—that's small and unpretentious—and ours with a wide, bright bay window facing east on the water.

The bay is pretty sheltered and it takes a lot of wind to make any kind of surf along our shore, but it was roaring in all right, so that the Richmonds' boat that was tied up to their dock and the Herrods', that lay in the slip next to it, were pitching, fore and aft, and their high riding lights bobbing bright and quick against the sky. The wind and the water were making so much noise I couldn't hear my own footsteps on the gravel, and it was so cloudy I didn't even see the two men standing in the dark of the lilac hedge near the Herrods' house. It just shows the state I was in that my throat got dry and there was goose flesh all over my arms when I heard their voices.

"I'm free to act as I see fit and I've told your pa so. That's all."

"Then you're quitting. Leaving us flat. Is that it?"

"It's none o' my doings. If your pa's riled at me because I'm fixing to do an act of kindness for a man that's got few enough to call on, it's his own look-out. There isn't much I stand to lose."

"Except your job."

"He can have my job—and welcome."

I knew who it was, then, of course, and I felt like a perfect It for being scared and pretty funny, too, because I'd been listening. I walked on, scuffing my feet so they'd hear me. But Les Herrod said in that flat, hard voice of his:

"The way things look, Arch'd be glad to take the trick for you," and then, "S-sh . . . somebody's coming."

Fred Mack turned and saw me and said, "It's only Kitty." He touched the brim of his old hat and said, "'Evening. You're a fine one to talk, Les Herrod. I've just about raised you from a pup and there's little enough I don't know about you. And I'll tell you right now, your brother can come along for all of me."

I said, "Good night," and went on and Les said, "What about Ruth? My brother's engaged to her."

"Well, what about her? She's a nice girl, but that butters no parsnips. If you hadn't been such a sniveling, mongrel whelp . . ."

I didn't hear any more, and I didn't want to hear any more. All I could think of was that before Alicia came, Sidley's Cove had been a friendly, easy-going place and people like Fred Mack were an institution—something you could count on the rest of your life to stick by you and not to change. And then she'd showed up and everything had gone wrong, and Sidley's Cove was divided against itself, the way Tess had said it would be, and the trouble was I wasn't even sure which side I was on.

It wasn't any help, of course, for Dad and Mother to get talking about Gerry Hunter after I got home. Not that it was their fault, goodness knows, because I started them.

I saw the light from the big lamp shining out through the bay window as soon as I'd passed Willoughbys' and it looked terribly good to me—warm and familiar—something I could count on, anyway. Mother was out in the kitchen piling up the last of the picnic things for Hilda to wash the next morning and Dad was in the living room, fixing himself a brandy. When I walked in he looked up with his nice, wise smile and said hello and did I want a little; he didn't think it would do me any harm, wasn't I cold? I said yes, I was, rather, even though I knew that wasn't really the reason why I was shivering. Mother came in and said was Tess all right and I said I'd dropped her off home and Mother wanted to know what on earth was the matter with that Gerald Hunter.

"Such a shock!" Mother said. "You'd think he'd see to her."

I've always told Mother she's spoiled, with Dad being the way he is about her, and that men don't make the same kind of fuss about girls now. I started to say something like that but Mother wouldn't have it.

"He made fuss enough over that . . ." I knew she'd been going to say "that Richmond girl" because it's what she'd called her, but then she caught herself and said instead, "the poor Richmond girl" and stopped.

I thought, Good heavens, is it going to keep on being like this? Is everybody going to keep on stumbling over her name and remembering how terribly she died, and having it all fall like a dead weight on people's thoughts and on everything they say or do? I simply couldn't go into it right then—and certainly not what I thought about Gerry and Arch and all that, so I began talking fast.

"It was really Mrs. Herrod's fault. You know how she orders things around. You could see for yourself how she practically took Gerry by the scruff of the neck and put him in their car with the rest of you. There wasn't much he could do about it without making a fuss."

"Henrietta," Dad said, "is too officious."

Henrietta is Mrs. Herrod and of course I thought so, too, but Mother'd never let me say anything against her from the time I was little. Besides, all of a sudden I wanted terribly to mention Mark's name just to see what they'd say. You know the way you do.

"Well, Tess was way off down the beach, someplace, and Mrs. Herrod knew I was going to drive Mark Crosby's car home . . ."

"I never did think much of him," Mother said.

It stopped me practically dead because I suppose I'd begun to realize how I felt about him myself and I think Mother's simply swell. I saw Dad looking at me over the tops of his glasses and I was absolutely sure there was a twinkle in his eyes. If it hadn't been for that I don't suppose I'd even have had the nerve to say, "Who?"

"That Gerald Hunter," Mother said.

"Oh!" I knew it must have been in a silly, faded sort of a way. "I thought you meant Mark."

"No. No, he seems all right. Though what he's doing up here . . ."

"He's having a vacation!" My voice sounded forced and rather wild, even to me. "Why on earth can't a detective have a vacation the way other people do?" And then I knew why I'd said it and there wasn't any doubt in my mind any longer about which side I was on.

"Postman's holiday." Dad smiled at me in the funny, wry way he used to when I was a little girl and had just been telling him it couldn't have been all that candy that had made me sick.

"I never thought much of him," Mother said over again, hanging on to her end of the conversation for dear life. "And I told Vinny Conover as much when Leslie first brought him up."

"Brought *who* up?" Of course Mother always knows what she's talking about, herself, but sometimes she gets pretty confusing to listen to and you just have to keep interrupting her if you ever hope to get things straight.

"Why, Gerald Hunter, of course. I told Vinny, right away that I wouldn't want my daughter running around with a man like that, but then Tess Conover always was headstrong—just like her mother—and neither one of them is exactly what I'd call conventional, either. Goodness knows, dear, I'm as fond of her as you are, but of course you couldn't help hearing something about it, though I will say for Leslie Herrod *he* never talked. Vinny just said she never held things against people—the past, I mean."

I could tell she was getting at something about Gerry Hunter and I wanted terribly to know what it was for my own sake and because of what Mark had asked me, too, but I knew I'd never get anything out of her if I let her go on like that.

"For heaven's sake, Mother. Will you stop talking riddles? What *is* it about Gerry?"

"Why, all that scandal," Mother said, "of course."

"What scandal?" I was positively breathless.

Dad said, "Now, Grace. Let sleeping dogs lie. He was pretty young at the time and, besides, we never got it straight. Only roundabout—talk . . ."

"If you want to call the Herrods roundabout!"

"*I* never heard anything!" I certainly didn't want them to get into one of their side tracks or I wouldn't hear anything now.

"No, my dear. It was several years ago. When; Leslie Herrod and Gerald Hunter were up at school. You were still going to bed at nine o'clock."

"Mother, please . . ."

Dad was looking over the tops of his glasses at Mother, and she said in a half-hearted sort of way, "Oh, he just got in some trouble over a girl at college and he was expelled for it. They didn't allow that sort of thing among under-graduates in those days."

"What on earth do you mean, *those* days? If you think they *allow* it now . . ."

"It was annulled," Mother said and then she looked at me in the most surprised way in the world. "I mean marriage, of course. Though what on earth that girl could have been thinking about . . ."

And I suddenly remembered the first time Les and Gerry came up after Alicia arrived. The day Mark Crosby came up, too. And how we'd driven along the road play-ing on those crazy harmonicas and had met Alicia and Mr. Richmond and let Mark out. And I remembered what Gerry had said and how he'd acted and then what Les had said in that short hard voice of his, too.

"Mother! Was the girl Alicia Richmond?"

"Now, Kitty!" Dad said. "Now, Mother! We don't know a thing about it. All we know it what the Herrods told us when Leslie brought Gerald Hunter up. If my opinion's worth a damn to either one of you, I think Henrietta Her-rod's capable of having made two-thirds of it up. And the less said about it now the better."

Dad was looking pretty tight-lipped along about then. He hates scandal and Mother wouldn't have kept on talking about it nearly as long as she did if I hadn't egged her on. But I simply had to know.

"Dad! Did Mrs. Herrod say the girl was Alicia Rich-mond?"

"Yes," he said. "Now run along."

I ran along all right. Fast. Up to my room where I could be by myself and think. Or try to think. But I couldn't think and I couldn't sleep, either. Everything kept going around and around in my head and I couldn't make head nor tail of it. I wondered how much Tess knew and if she was trying to shield Gerry in taking the blame on herself. Because all of a sudden I remembered that it was Gerry who had been on his feet saying, "I'll give her my coat," and going toward Alicia first. And I wondered if Tess had seen anything the rest of us hadn't that had made her grab Arch's hand and Ruth's and pull them up and make them run across the beach with her.

But that didn't make sense either. Because, if Gerry had been so much in love with Alicia when he was in school that he had married her and had fallen in love with her all over again when he saw her this summer, he certainly wouldn't have wanted to kill her. Not unless he was crazy-jealous over the way she was playing up to Arch. And even then, you'd think it would have been Arch he'd have picked on instead.

I couldn't do anything with it and I kept thinking about how I had to see Tess tomorrow and tell her what Mark Crosby had said and how I'd promised him to drive Gerry Hunter and Les to the station for the noon train and see what I could get out of Gerry. And I wondered how much Mark really knew that he hadn't told me. I turned back and forth in bed until the sheets were all hot and wrinkled and I heard the birds beginning to jabber and I saw that it was getting light. I got up and smoothed the sheets and turned the top covers back over the foot of the bed so that they would air for a little while and I went over to the window, and stood looking out.

It was peaceful and calm and cool out there with the bay shining like pewter in the early light, and the pine trees smelled sharp and exciting the way they had when I was a little girl. I heard a truck coming along the road and I remembered when Bill Hennebery used to deliver the milk with a horse and wagon and then before that when

you had to go down to the store for it with a covered pail
and how I'd see Fred Mack down there sometimes and he'd
let me go over his fishing boat and had even taken me out
for a trip on it a few times. Everything was all right then,
I thought. People were decent to each other and you knew
who belonged to who and there wasn't ever any trouble.

The truck came to a stop in front of our house and Bill
Hennebery got out and came up the driveway and I heard
him set the milk bottles down on the kitchen porch and
then go along the path that runs in back of the cottages, the way he always does, to the Conovers' next door. I
was thinking how he had looked just like a silhouette of
a milkman, with his carrier and bottles and even the way
he walked, cut out of black paper in the gray, early light.
And I heard him set the bottles down on the Conovers'
steps and go clanking on again to Willoughbys' and Herrods' and the Greene place. And then a door slammed and
I could hear men's voices, very low, and three people came
along the road together to where the truck was parked.

One of them was Bill with his empty carrier and I could
see the others were men, too, and they were both carrying
suitcases. For a minute it didn't make any sense at all, and
then I saw them get up into the truck beside Bill and all of
a sudden I knew that it was Les Herrod and Gerry Hunter
and that Bill must be driving them over to Thornton to
catch the early morning train.

8

It was a perfectly terrible day, all through. I didn't really go to sleep after that, but just dozed off, and all the morning noises on the bay kept waking me up. The wind had dropped in the night, but there were still some rollers coming in along the shore and every single youngster in Sidley's Cove must have gone in swimming before breakfast. I don't suppose I would have blamed them if I hadn't been so jumpy and sunk for sleep because it was the hottest weather yet, but I didn't see why on earth they had to pick this morning, of all times, to yell from one end of the beach to the other and do all their kid dives flat and screaming.

Then when I did manage to go sound asleep for a little around seven, Mother called up to me in her most cheerful voice that breakfast was nearly ready and Hilda was doing blueberry muffins and I didn't want to miss them while they were warm, did I? I said, "O. K." and dragged myself out of bed and gave one look at myself in the mirror and decided it didn't matter what I put on, and then a motor began to cut and splutter, and I looked out and saw Fred Mack just coming up out of the cabin of the Richmonds' *Lark*.

Well, I thought, let him, but I kept wondering all through breakfast what on earth he was tuning that up for with Alicia lying dead in their house, and Mother said I'd better stop fretting or I'd make myself sick. And I knew I had to get hold of Mark as soon as I could and tell him everything and get it off my mind.

Which was a whole lot easier said than done because of course I couldn't march right up to the Richmonds' where he was staying and ask for him point blank—not with the way things were. And I wanted to see Tess, too, but not until after I'd talked to Mark and asked him whether he thought I should let Tess know I'd seen Gerry and Des get into that truck and drive away early like that with Bill Hennebery.

I knew if I sat on the beach I'd be sure to see Mark sooner or later because the Greene place is farther out toward the point than ours is and he'd have to go past me even if he only went to the store. So I put on the coolest dress I could find and a big, floppy hat and picked up a book I'd been trying to read and went out.

I couldn't see anybody at first because all the kids had had breakfast and their mothers wouldn't let them go in the water again until ten o'clock. That's one of the things about Sidley's Cove—you can just about tell what time it is by what people are doing. Even something as upsetting as Alicia's death doesn't really throw the routine out. Like Mother's planning blueberry muffins for breakfast and waking me up to eat them.

The *Felicity* was moored beside the Herrods' dock, and I remember thinking how neglected she had been looking ever since Fred Mack had lined up with the Richmonds and how that must have made the Herrods pretty mad. And then Fred came up on deck again on the *Lark*. I'd always liked Fred and he'd been kind of fond of me, too, ever since I was a little kid, and what I'd heard him say the night before to Les had been one of the things that had kept me awake worrying. I went on up the road and across the beach to the Richmonds' dock. Fred was swabbing the decks, and his ducks were rolled up to his wiry, old calves, and the water sloshing all around his feet. I don't know whether it was because it made it look so slippery, or what, that I all of a sudden said:

"Fred, can you swim?"

"Not if I can help it."

"No, but really . . ."

He had the same kind of teasing look in his eyes he had had when I was a little girl and used to ask him questions all the time about everything.

"I guess I could paddle a spell," he said, "if I was put to it." He stooped and dropped his bucket into the water over the low stern rail and pulled it up again, full, and poured it over the deck so that it ran fast and clean down the scuppers. "I'm not aiming, though," he said, "to be put to it."

He smiled at me just the way he did when I was little, and it was so natural that all of a sudden things seemed all right again the way they used to be. When you get light-hearted, sometimes, you get careless. At least I do. And I suppose I was pretty groggy, too, from not having had much sleep and thinking about things so much. Anyway, I was really just talking for something to say and didn't give it a second thought.

"What are you cleaning her up for, Fred?"

His face changed so fast it scared me. He was a big man and strong and of course he was tanned and weathered so his blue eyes were rather startling, anyway, staring out of his dark skin. I remember I used to be afraid of him when I was a very little girl and before I got to know him. I was afraid of him now.

"So it'll be a fit place," he said, scowling, "for her to rest in." He jerked his head sideways toward the cabin. "She's in there now," he said. "I'm standing watch to keep her safe."

The way he said it and then knowing it, too, made me feel creepy all up my spine. And then, just standing there, talking to Fred like that . . .

"Oh . . ." I said, "oh . . . Alicia . . ."

His mouth twisted in the slow way it used to when he was putting me straight over something dumb I'd asked about his boat. "Remember?" he said. "She's dead!"

"Oh Fred! I know. I'm sorry. It's just that I've been thinking about it all night—thinking in circles and I guess I must have come to the place where I had to stop thinking about it or go crazy . . . Fred!" I was wound up and I kept right on. "Fred, what were you and Leslie Herrod quarreling about last night?" I saw him wait a minute as if he meant to tell me to mind my own business, but I guess he was pretty unhappy about things, and he probably wanted to get some of it off his chest, too.

"I wouldn't call that any quarrel." He leaned over the side and dipped up another bucket of water. "I give him a piece o' my mind. That's all. It's past due."

"Oh, but Fred, I heard you call him . . ."

"Yep, and it's maybe a good thing you come along when you did or I'd a' called him a whole lot worse." He pushed the water over the boards with his deck swab. "I suppose you're like all the rest o' them—figure it's her fault. Well, it's not. It's theirs." He jerked his head inshore and I knew what he meant. He meant the Herrods. "All except Arch. He's the only one in that family's all right. He's fixing to go along."

"What?" I couldn't believe it.

Fred's eyes were hard and blue and his mouth was set in a grim, hard line.

"Arch is going along."

"On the boat? With you and Mr. Richmond and . . . Alicia?"

"Yep!"

"Oh, Fred . . ."

"What's the matter with that?"

"Oh, Fred, isn't there enough trouble now?"

"No more'n there's been all along. Time it was cleared out. Your friend, there . . ." I felt the blood rush up, warm, into my face because he jerked his head in the direction of the Greene place and I knew he was talking about Mark. "Your friend's doing all he can."

I looked up the sloping lawn to the house, hoping to see Mark I suppose, and for the first time I noticed that there was a car there that wasn't the Richmonds' or the Fiat, either, standing in the driveway. I don't know why, but I didn't like it.

"Who's that?"

"Brownlow and Stewart. The sheriff and the prosecutor're trying to nose out trouble—stir up things more'n they are now. He'll fix 'em, though." Fred looked mighty satisfied, I thought. "He'll tie 'em up in a knot they can't untie till he's ready to do it for 'em."

"Who?" I said. "Mark?"

Fred gave me a funny look. "Oh, so it's Mark with you, is it? Well that's all right . . ."

I heard the door open and I saw Mark, and Steve Brownlow and Art Stewart come out and stand talking to him on the porch. After a minute or two they got into their car and Mark got in with them and they came down the driveway and turned south toward town and Mark waved at me as they went by.

It certainly left me at loose ends. I couldn't settle down to anything and it seemed as though everybody in Sidley's Cove except the little kids and me had just plain vanished. I wandered back to the beach, but not even Ruth or Helen showed up, and when I finally made up my mind I'd just go and see Tess without waiting to talk to Mark first, Mrs. Conover told me Tess was in bed and she didn't want to disturb her. She hadn't slept much, poor dear, after that

frightful experience and she'd just dozed off and I understood, didn't I?

I almost told her about how I'd seen Gerry and Les
sneak off like that—because, of course, it's all you could
call it—but I thought maybe I'd better keep quiet until I
knew how things stood. I kept wondering if Tess knew and
feeling terribly sorry for her and pretty mad at Gerry and
thinking there was something, after all, in what Mother
had said about the way he treated her.

I went in swimming at ten o'clock the way I usually did
but I was all alone except for the little kids and after I'd
played around with them for a while, trying to teach Connie Arnold how to do a decent back dive, I drifted up to
the house and ate lunch. By the middle of the afternoon I
was fit to be tied, and then just as I was walking down to
the store because I thought I'd heard the mail train whistle
in, Mark came along in the Fiat and picked me up.

I was so glad I could have cried and I suppose I must
have looked it because when he pulled up in front of the
store he said:

"Don't let yourself get in such a stew, youngster. These
things take time."

He went in and collected the mail and came out again
and said, "What you need's to get away from the whole
bunch for a little. We'll take a run out to the end of the
point through the woods. You've been messing around with
too many people and they've got on your nerves."

"Oh, Mark," I said, "I don't know what on earth to do.
Everybody I've ever known and liked is acting funny."

"Keep right on liking 'em," he said.

"But Mark, they're having trouble."

"All the more reason for sticking to 'em."

And then I told him all about Fred Mack and Les and
what Fred had said about Arch's going along on the boat
when Mr. Richmond took Alicia's body down.

"Yes," Mark said, "I know. I don't like it."

"Neither do I. Can't you do anything about it?"

"I'm going to try," he said. "I'm going to do what I can."

He drove out along the bay road and through the woods to the end of the point where you look out on open water and the breakers come in, white and foaming, over a long sand bar. When he'd parked the car and we'd sat quiet for a little, I felt better and I told him everything.

All about how Gerry Hunter had been kicked out of school for marrying Alicia and how thinking about it had kept me awake and how I'd seen Gerry and Les Herrod get into the truck with Bill Hennebery before daylight so I knew they must have caught the early morning train.

He listened without even asking me a question and when I'd finished he was frowning.

"Didn't you know that," I said, "about Gerry and Alicia?"

"No. No, I didn't know it."

"I'd think Mr. Richmond would have told you that himself. After what's happened."

"No. Nobody told me that. I'm no end grateful to you for having dug it out. Thanks a lot."

He was acting awfully funny, it seemed to me. I'd been wanting so terribly to talk to him, because I'd thought he could straighten things out and make me feel better about them, but instead he was being absolutely dead pan and I couldn't get a rise out of him at all.

"But aren't you terribly surprised," I said, "that they left early like that? Sneaking away before anybody could get a chance to say a word to them?"

"After what's happened," he said, and I looked up quick to see if he was mocking me but I couldn't even tell by his expression whether he was or not, "I'm not at all surprised. In fact, I'd have been more surprised if they hadn't. Particularly as there's a letter here, postmarked a hundred miles or so down state, that I strongly suspect of being from Hunter himself."

"For you?" I said. I thought he was crazy. "Why on earth haven't you read it, then?"

"Wanted to get the story from you first. That's proba-bly the way Hunter figured it would hit me and I usually try to oblige. Helps me in my work. Go out with the tide of the other fellow's mind and come back in with your own."

He opened it and took out a folded sheet of paper and read the note, and handed it to me.

You could see it had been written on the train, of course, because the handwriting was so shaky. There wasn't any date and no salutation. It just said:

"If you know what's good for you, Crosby, get out of this. I'll see you in town any time you want, but unless I'm extradited I'm not going to talk for what calls itself the law up there. For God's sake, let sleeping dogs lie."

It was signed, "Gerald C. Hunter," and I remembered I'd never heard anybody but my mother call him Gerald and I remembered, too, what Dad had said about sleep-ing dogs. I gave the note back to Mark and he sat there for simply ages, not saying a word. I kept glancing at my watch every little while, but the way he was looking, as though he'd forgotten I was on earth and wouldn't have cared anyway, I didn't dare open my mouth. Honestly, it was nearly an hour before he came out of it. When he did, he smiled at me and said, "Hello, Kathie!" and stepped on the starter and drove slowly back along the bay shore road.

"Well," he said, "that's that."

"What's what?"

"Remember a story that made a lot of headlines a few years, ago? *Carwood Thrill Killer Case,* I think the tabloids called it. About a man who did two jobs—murder—just for the fun of seeing the stuff in print?"

"Yes. Yes, of course. He was caught, wasn't he, trying to commit a third?"

"Right! Trapped himself—with a little help from me. I was handling the case, you know, for Mrs. Carwood. Her husband had been the second person murdered in a pretty close group.

"Had a quirk in him—the killer. Thought he wasn't appreciated, all that sort of thing, and just started out to make the world sit up and take notice. Got a big kick out of reading about all the trouble he was stirring up and nobody suspecting him.

"Well, I got co-operation—newspapers and law, both—and the story was dropped like a hot cake. Not a word about it after the first two days. Took the kick right out of his reading matter. Then I waited on his old stamping ground for him to react. He did—fast—couldn't stand the obscurity."

"Mark! Do you think there's somebody like that behind Alicia's death?"

"Well—something like that, anyway. Not exactly, perhaps—one murder never really duplicates another, but I've been hoping I could play the same game, and the cards are being dealt right into my hand. If Dr. Carver—he's coroner, you know—hadn't turned in a report of 'accidental death' on Alicia . . ."

"Oh really, Mark? When?" It made me feel terribly relieved and awfully upset, too, for some silly reason, all at the same time.

"Today—not fifteen minutes before I picked you up. Which was swell, because of course there wasn't much left for the sheriff and the prosecutor to do but fall in line. And then this business of Hunter's clearing out—and writing that letter . . . yes, things are shaping fine."

"Mark! What are you going to do? About Gerry, I mean."

"Nothing. Not a thing! Don't you worry about Hunter, Kathie. He'll show up all right when the time's ripe."

9

I remember the next thing I thought was that the way Mr. Richmond acted about Alicia's death was pretty funny. Of course I knew that some of it was because Mark told him to, but even so . . .

You see, Sidley's Cove has always stuck together whenever anything important has come up, and Mr. Richmond stuck with Sidley's Cove. Which was just the trouble, because everybody expected him to turn against it after that. A lot of people who had been pretty mad about his taking the Greene place to begin with and the high-handed way he picked Fred Mack off thought he was just a little too quick about being willing to hush things up. Mother got kind of tight-lipped over it, and the Willoughbys came right out and said he didn't act the way they expected a father to—Alicia being his only child and all that. And then the Herrods . . . Mrs. Conover was the only person who stood up for him except Arch, of course, and Fred Mack. And then I didn't know how Mark really felt about it, either, for a long time.

You see, I'd made up my mind which side I was on and that Mark was absolutely all right no matter how things seemed, but it wasn't any too easy, sometimes, sticking to it. Like when he told me I'd been a lot of help to him and would I mind keeping my eyes and ears open some more

in a place or two where it was important. At first I was
pretty horrified.

"I can't *do* things like that," I said. "Spy on people . . ."

"What do you think you've been doing so far?"

"Oh! About Tess, you mean, and what my folks told me
about Gerry? But I thought you ought to know."

"So I ought. And there's probably a lot of other things
I ought to know, too. But I can't be everyplace, and people won't tell me a lot of things they will you or talk as
freely when I'm around. You know, Kathie, whatever else I
think about Gerry Hunter—and I'll be honest and tell you
I'm not at all sure what I think in certain directions right
now—I'm in agreement with him on one thing and that is
that there's a sleeping dog here. Only I'm not the fellow
to let it lie."

He took my hand and held it for a minute, and I knew
that I didn't care what happened if only he would be
around, once in a while, to help soften the bumps.

"I'm not going to let it lie because I've got something
more than a hunch that it's Cerberus to a hell of a lot of
facts that lead to Alicia's death—Alicia's murder."

"Oh!" I said and I know my voice sounded awfully
shaky because though I'd known, really, that that's what
he thought it was, he hadn't actually called it that before.

"Murder! Good, straight, first-degree murder."

"Tess?" I said, pretty scared. "Gerry?" In another minute I was going to cry.

"No," he said. "Not Tess. Though how much she knows
about it . . . And as for Gerald Hunter, well . . . All I
know is that it was murder, not manslaughter. Somebody
planned it—nice and deliberate and well thought out. At
least that's my opinion. But I've got to prove it and I've got
to find out who, and what's more I've got to find out how.
And I'm asking you to help me by holding your chin up
and keeping your eyes and ears open for what other people

say and do, and your blessed little mouth shut about what I've just told you. Because there's a smooth bird working this game—or a desperate one—and the more he thinks I'm just running around the country amusing myself, the better. The way I size things up I've got to work fast and watch my step or I'll walk right into it with my eyes shut. And I'm not at all sure I'll be the only one. If I don't find out who and exactly why and at least pretty much how mighty soon there's going to be more than one accidental death in Sidley's Cove this summer, or I miss my guess."

"Oh!" I said, holding my chin up as well as I could.

"There! All my cards are on your table. You can see for yourself that I've got to cover ground and cover it quick. And you covered ground for me in that one little chit-chat with your father and mother that I couldn't have covered in a month of Sundays. That's why you've got to keep on being eyes and ears for me in places where, if I were around, there wouldn't be anything either to see or hear. If you're willing, that is."

By that time I was glad that I'd decided, the night before, which side I was on. Because Mark's pretty impulsive, for all he's so level-headed, and if I had hesitated I think he might very well have said, "O. K." and gone on without me. Which would have been absolutely terrible because goodness knows where it would all have ended. Not that I wasn't dumb about what I found out, but the important thing is that I did find things out and told Mark about them. And of course he isn't dumb at all.

Anyway, I said, "All right, I'll do what I can," and he said, "Good girl," and told me.

"Mr. Richmond is sure, too, that Alicia was murdered, Kathie. But he's going to put on an act for the community. Drag a red herring across the trail. Understand?"

"Yes," I said, but I didn't exactly. Not until he told me some more, anyway.

"Do you suppose you could manage to be around within earshot of a conversation that's set to take place in the Herrods' living room in about half an hour?"

"Goodness!" I said. "I don't know."

"Because I'd like a disinterested witness to judge how the Herrods take it when Mr. Richmond tells them he doesn't want Arch along on that trip."

"Oh . . ." And then it dawned, "That's swell!"

"I don't know how swell it's going to be. Depends on how it works. But you can see for yourself that Richmond, at this point, isn't capable of being particularly objective about the whole thing. He'll do well if he doesn't break down. And I certainly can't count on him for impressions—how they take it and what they say. But I can count on you. You've got a natural flair for reporting, though you probably never thought of it like that."

"No." I could feel myself getting red right up to the roots of my hair because, whatever anybody else might think about it—my family, for instance—I knew that, coming from him, it was a whale of a compliment.

"You know the lay of the land, Kitty. Maybe you can figure out some way to hear without being seen."

"I could play tennis," I said. "The Herrods' court is right outside their living-room windows."

"Where they could see you," he said, grinning at me, "plain as day."

"Where I can keep an eye on the path until Mr. Richmond shows up."

"Then what?"

"Then I'll clear out . . ." I was trying to think and talk at the same time. "And head for home . . . and come back to the Herrods' along the path through the woods."

"All right. So far, so good."

"There's a bench," I said, rushing the words out because I was excited and I really did have an idea, "that faces the court. It's sort of—a spectator's bench for when you're not playing tennis but just watching, or between games. It's set in a clump of lilacs near the house—right up close to the living-room windows. They can't see you from inside but you can hear. I know . . ." and I could feel my face getting all hot again when I remembered and thought about how I'd be intentionally doing something this time that I'd gone out of my way to keep from doing before—"I know because I got up and left it one day when I overheard the Herrods arguing."

"What were they arguing about?"

"I don't know. Something about Les . . . I tell you, I didn't listen. It seems to me . . . listening isn't very nice!"

He could tell, of course, that I was getting jittery over doing the whole thing, when I really thought about it. The way he looked at me was quick and cold.

"Neither is murder," he said.

"All right, Mark." There was a lump in my throat and I had to blink my eyes to keep the tears back. "It isn't easy."

"No, Kitty . . . no. I'm sorry. You're being swell. And you're plan's swell, too, except for one thing."

"What?" I'd thought it was pretty fool-proof myself because the way the lilac hedge runs along the side of the house I knew I could get to the bench without anybody's seeing me from the living room.

"Who's going to be your obliging partner in all this? Who's going to be just tickled to death to play tennis with you for as long as you want to play—which will be until Richmond shows up—and then be equally tickled to stop right then and there—in the middle of a game, maybe, and go away and not bother you any more?"

But I was ready for him on that one. I'd thought it all out.

"Connie Arnold!" I said. "She'd break her neck to play tennis with one of us older ones. Besides, I'm teaching her to do a back dive."

"O. K," Mark was still laughing at me when he drove off.

Of course we all played tennis on the Herrods' court. We always had. Nobody thought anything of it if you played there with somebody besides Arch or Leslie, but that didn't mean I didn't feel pretty self-conscious, knowing what I was up to, out there with Connie who was ten and just learning. Not that I hadn't played tennis with the little kids lots of times but the way I was brought up it's a major crime to listen to somebody else's conversation—like opening their letters and all that. It seemed to me that anybody must have seen it sticking out all over me that I was beginning to feel like Mata Hari or something.

Anyway, it shot my game so that Connie won the set 6–4 and she was squealing, "Game *and* set, Kitty! Game *and* set!" when Mr. Richmond rounded the drive and came walking up the path toward Herrods' house.

He waved at me and I tried to smile back but all I could think of was that he was looking as though he didn't have a care in the world and not like a man whose only daughter had just died suddenly and pretty terribly and who wasn't even buried yet. And somehow, all of a sudden, it struck me that maybe what Mark really wanted was to know how Mr. Richmond acted and what he said and that he didn't care about the Herrods much at all.

"That's all, Connie," I said. "Time to swim."

"O-oh, Kitty . . . ple-ease . . . let's not stop now."

"Play you tomorrow," I said.

Connie's really a good kid and anyway she was feeling pretty swell, of course, about having beaten me. She only said, "ple-ease . . ." once more, and when I shook my head and picked up the balls and started to leave the court she said, "All right, Kitty. See you on the beach," and ran off toward home.

I had an awful time making myself walk slow while I was still in sight of the Herrods' windows, and when I knew I was hidden by the pines I ran as fast as I could make it down the road to our house and around back and along the woods path to where the Herrods' lilac hedge begins. It's an old one that's been there since long before I was born, I guess, so it's plenty tall enough to hide me, but I suppose I was self-conscious about what I was doing anyway and I was stooping a little when I rounded the clump where the bench is sheltered. You can imagine how I felt when I saw Arch sitting there.

I put my hand up to my mouth quick, to keep from making any sound. Arch had a funny, ironic twist to the corners of his mouth and he looked straight at me and then moved over on the bench to make room for me beside him. And neither of us said a word.

10

I thought, Oh, my heavens! Arch knows. He knows what Mr. Richmond's come about and he knows that I know. And he's going to make trouble.

"Arch," I said, quite low, but his hand closed tight on my wrist.

"Be quiet," he whispered. "Spies can't be too careful."

A door closed and voices came faintly from the hall. They grew louder and you could hear Arch's father and mother and Mr. Richmond coming into the living room, though you couldn't quite make out what they were saying. Then suddenly, right close to the window, Mrs. Herrod said, in that deep, booming voice of hers:

"Well, Charles . . ."

Of course I'd never heard any of them call him anything but Mr. Richmond from the first, and the way she said it you couldn't help realizing that she knew him a whole lot better than she had ever admitted all along.

"Well, Henrietta . . ."

"Charles, we want you to know we're sorry, genuinely sorry." It was Mr. Herrod, fussy and nervous, the way he was about half the time, and I could just see him in there, looking henpecked and talking fast so he could get it in before his wife had time to interrupt him.

"Thank you, Jim. That sounds—good—coming from you."

Mr. Richmond was pleasant enough, but the way he used the words made them sound as though they were a handful of stones that he was throwing in Mr. Herrod's face. I didn't like it. It made me terribly unhappy and I was beginning to get frightened, too. Mr. Richmond cleared his throat.

"It occurred to me that you might like to know, Henrietta, that Dr. Carver's official opinion is that Alicia's death was accidental."

"Well!" Every time Mrs. Herrod said anything her voice came out as though she was at the sending end of a loud speaker. "That's fine, isn't it? Very nice of Dr. Carver, I'm sure."

"There was some question"—Mr. Richmond sounded a little apologetic, it seemed to me—"for a while, at least . . ."

"Indeed! And who, may I ask, raised the question?"

"Dr. Carver."

"Dr. Carver," Mrs. Herrod was pretty acid, "Dr. Carver has a reputation for being a very good country practitioner. Personally, I wouldn't call him in for a sick dog."

"No, I suppose not. However, his reputation is growing. Becoming a little more than local. He's been making a study, the last year or two, of legal medicine. In any case, I had no choice. He's coroner, you know."

"As it happens, I didn't. May I remind you, Charles, that I've never had any occasion . . ."

"Now, Henrietta!" It was Mr. Herrod again, trying to smooth things over. The only place I'd ever seen him show any honest-to-goodness spunk was when he bossed his children. And even then, it was Mrs. Herrod who had really done the bossing.

"Don't 'Now, Henrietta' me, James. I want Charges Richmond to tell me just one thing and that is, does he intend to stay around here where he's not wanted even after this?"

"Why," Mr. Richmond said in his friendliest and most reasonable voice, "should I go away?"

"You did before. After the last—shall we agree to call it 'accident' again, Charles?"

"Henrietta!"

But nothing was stopping Henrietta now that she had the bit in her teeth.

"I have no idea why Charles Richmond ever had the monstrous effrontery—simply monstrous—to come back here in the first place after all these years. And if he has half the sense I assume he was born with, he'll get out again—fast—and stay out this time."

Mr. Richmond had been just too courteous and pleasant all the way through. It seemed to me that if anybody had talked to me that way, right in my face, I'd have been pretty mad. He didn't even raise his voice, though. He simply said:

"I've bought the Greene place."

"Yes, I know. After all, Leslie is in Mr. Greene's office. Well, sell it again. James will buy it from you. He's been intending to for quite a while. For Arch . . ."

She stopped as though she had just realized how far things had gone and how it looked now as though Arch would certainly never want the Greene place for himself and Ruth. I looked at Arch quick but he'd gone absolutely dead pan.

"I didn't come here," Mr. Richmond was saying, "to quarrel with you, Henrietta. About the Greene place or anything else. I came to talk with you about your son."

"We will not discuss my son!"

"About Arch . . ." The way Mr. Richmond said it made me think of somebody who was patient and resigned about trying to brush a buzzing fly away. "Arch is determined to go . . ."

Mrs. Herrod had been so lofty and superior about everything and now all of a sudden, she sounded beaten and scared. "Arch! What about Arch? Isn't it enough that that—that girl . . ."

I caught my breath because of course I knew she was talking about Alicia and I thought, How on earth can Mr. Richmond stand there like that and take it? But his voice didn't even change.

"It seemed to me that you'd better know that Arch has made up his mind he's going along down with us on the boat when we take Alicia home. And that it's not any of my doing."

There wasn't a sound in that room for what I thought must be at least a whole minute. Then Mr. Herrod said in a funny, choked voice,

"Arch . . ."

But Mrs. Herrod was right in there before he could do anything more with it.

"Of course Arch isn't going with you! The very idea! Is the boy out of his head?"

I was wishing with all my heart that I could put my arms around Arch and hold him tight and still for a little—just for a little until things had time to quiet down. Until he was cooler and calmer himself, and all the people in there who were so angry and upset—all except Mr. Richmond who was acting altogether too smooth and controlled—had time to get hold of themselves, too. But I couldn't do a thing. I couldn't stop Arch from jumping up from the bench and pushing his way through the lilac hedge and going straight into the house through the French windows and saying,

"I'm going, Mother."

"Arch . . . !" I could hear the quick way she drew in her breath before she said it. "Arch—you've been listening!"

"Never mind about that. I'm going with Mr. Richmond."

"You'll do as I say."

"I'm going. I'm not a boy. I'm a reasonably adult male."

"Without an income!"

"Not entirely. I earn a few dollars now and then."

"Precious few! Daubing . . ."

"O. K. But I'm going."

All the stubbornness that Arch got from his mother, and that was just a fine steadiness and loyalty when nobody stood in the way of his doing something he had made up his mind to do, was up in him now, and I knew things were going to be pretty bad.

"Fred Mack's getting old. He can't run that boat alone, and Mr. Richmond doesn't know a thing about a motor. Pardon me, sir, but it's true, isn't it?"

That was the place, I thought, for Mr. Richmond to have stepped in and told Arch himself, to his face, that he didn't want him to go. It's the only thing, probably, that would have stopped him. And I was so mad at Mr. Richmond I couldn't see straight for the kindly, affectionate way he said:

"Yes, my boy, it's true enough, and mighty fine of you, but . . ."

Of course that's all Arch needed. "Thank you," he said. "You can count on me."

"You don't know what you're talking about, Arch Herrod! You don't know what you're doing." Mrs. Herrod's voice was pitched so high it was nearly a scream. "Taking sides against your own family. You don't know all that's happened."

"I know enough. It's about time somebody took the other side."

"The other side! There is no other side." I thought, my heavens, if *she* gets hysterical . . . "Charles Richmond, if you ask me, you're as callous and indifferent about the death of your daughter as you were about the death of your wife."

"Henrietta . . ." The way Mr. Herrod said it was getting weaker and weaker as though he had finally decided to give it all up and just let her go.

"I'll say what I think, James. You know perfectly well when I realized that—the girl was dead, you said it seemed to you that it was mighty coincidental—altogether too coincidental."

"Poor child . . ."

"Poor child, indeed! Of course you'd say 'poor child.' What is there left for you to say? James Herrod, you're the worst hypocrite I've ever . . ."

I couldn't stand any more of it. It simply wasn't in me to stay out there listening to people I'd known all my life saying things like that to each other, telling me things about themselves that only made a jumble in my mind but that I knew were terrible, just the same. If everybody in Sidley's Cove was going to die, I thought, because I hadn't stayed to hear the rest, I couldn't help it. And besides, none of it made sense. Mr. Richmond was acting funny; there wasn't any doubt about that, and, if Mrs. Herrod knew things about him that Mark didn't know, maybe it was time he learned them, too.

I got up from the bench and crossed the court fast, not even bothering to care whether they saw me or not from the windows. I was remembering that Mark had said Mr. Richmond hadn't told him anything about Alicia and Gerry Hunter, and I was sure now that the real reason he had wanted me to listen was not so much to find out how the Herrods took Mr. Richmond's visit as to learn what Mr. Richmond did and said himself! Maybe he wasn't even sure that the man who was his host was telling him the truth, and of course somebody like me was the only way he'd have of finding anything like that out. I was so terribly upset I didn't even look where I was going and I almost ran into the Fiat before I saw it, with Mark sitting there behind the wheel.

It was parked off the road in the shade of the lilacs and he opened the door for me and held out his hand. I was breathing pretty fast, I guess, from running and being so excited and miserable and all.

"There now," he said, "just take your time. I have to run into the village to deliver a message to Bertha Mack for Fred. You come along with me and tell me all about it." He smiled that wide, warm smile and I began to feel better just because of it.

"I know. The world's turned upside down and everything's tumbled around your head and you're scared stiff. But you'll get over it. Honest you will. You see, I know, Kathie, what happens when you run slam bang into a sleeping dog and it wakes up and growls. But that doesn't mean it's showing its teeth at *you*."

11

I felt a lot better, of course, when I'd told Mark all about
it on the way back from the Macks' house. I'd waited for
him out in the car while he ran up the steps and knocked
and Bertha Mack opened the door a minute and I saw her
long, solemn face that used to bother me when I was a kid,
peering out at him. I knew he'd just come to tell her that
Fred was going down on the boat and wouldn't be home
for four or five days, and I saw her nod and shut the door,
and he came down the steps and climbed in and started up
the car again.

Later, when things broke, I remembered that as we
drove away I thought I heard her call out to him again
but I wasn't sure, and, anyway, I figured it wasn't anything
important after all. Which just goes to show . . .

Not that he cleared anything up for me. In fact, after
I got through talking, I was even more puzzled than I had
been before because of the way he took it all. It's only that
I was trusting him, even then, more than I'd ever trusted
anybody in my life except my folks and I felt that whatever he did was all right. Still, it was funny to watch him
sitting there nodding when I told him all that about Mr.
Richmond.

"I think maybe it's a good thing I listened. Because it's
probably something you ought to know."

"Yes. Thanks." And I saw the corners of his eyes were crinkled.

"Well, you don't have to laugh at me. I really did think . . ."

"I'm not laughing at you, Kathie. Honest, I'm not. I'm laughing at how smart people think they are and how dumb they usually succeed in being. Every last person in that room today was playing a game and they all thought they were putting it over on the others. And none of than was. Except Richmond. He was putting something over all right."

"Yes," I said. "That's what I thought."

"Only, he wasn't putting anything over on me. Get that straight."

"Then he's been lying to you all along! Is that it? He's been keeping things from you and trying to pull the wool over your eyes. Isn't that true, Mark? You're going to tell him, aren't you? You aren't going to stick with him after this?"

"No. I'm not going to tell him anything. And as for sticking with him—I think it's the best thing I could possibly do. That is, if I want to get anyplace in clearing this mess up. Listen, Kathie, that dog that growled and scared the daylights out of you is guarding a nice, quiet skeleton in somebody's closet. Before I get through I'm going to open the door and let it tumble out."

"Mark," I said, "do you know anything I don't know?"

He simply roared, throwing his head back and laughing till I wanted to shake him. When he stopped finally he took both my hands in his and held them tight and looked at me with his terribly kind, humorous brown eyes.

"I'm sorry," he said. "Honest I am. And you've got to believe me that I'm not laughing at you. Not really. It's only that you're so all-fired solemn and swell about it all. And loyal and good. That's what you are, Kathie—you're good. And I want you to know one thing: I won't let you down. Ever! Understand?"

His voice had gone all deep, and the way he looked at me I was blinking, trying to keep the tears out of my eyes because it made me so happy and so sad, too, at the same time.

"Oh Mark," I said, "I think you're swell. And I'm back of you—all the way."

"O. K." He let my hands go and went back to talking in that funny, easy-going way of his that always had a laugh behind it. "Sure I know something you don't know. I know a whole lot of things you don't know and that other people don't know. That's my business. To be a receiving point for information from a lot of different sources.

"You see, one person knows one thing—Mr. Richmond, for instance—and another person knows another—Gerry, or the Herrods—and sometimes several people know something, but they only know it from one side of the fence—their own. When anything like this happens—when trouble breaks and a fellow like me is asked to stick around—it's my business to try to collect all the things everybody knows on both sides of the fence. That's one reason why I wanted you to listen in today—because the two sets of people with opposing stories were being forced to meet on common ground. The ground, in this instance, happening to be Arch. And I wanted to know how they both took it."

"The way Mr. Richmond is taking Alicia's death," I said, and I know I must have sounded exactly like my mother, "is something I don't like."

"A lot of other people don't like it, too. It worries 'em."

"Is that why he's doing it? On purpose?"

Mark smiled. "Make what you can of it. I didn't say a word."

We had reached the beach in front of our house by that time and Mark said:

"There's Tess. You might give a look at how she's taking things today."

"Mark! Tess is my best friend. I can't spy on her."

"Not even to help her out? Have you forgotten, already, what I told you? That I'm a receiving point for information so things can get straightened out? Tess is in trouble, Kathie. Or thinks she is. And Gerry. . ."

"All right." He opened the door and let me out and I went down across the sand to where Tess was sitting.

"Hello, Kitty. Coming in?" She was looking perfectly awful.

"I haven't got my suit."

"Go and get it then." I felt so sorry for her I could have cried, and I went on up to the house as fast as I could and changed and came back down. She was lying there, all alone, on the beach, scooping up sand in little, vicious digs with a piece of broken shell.

"Oh, Tess," I said, "I'm sorry . . ."

"Thanks."

"No, but really . . . I mean, it must be simply awful, being in love with somebody and having him clear out like that without saying good-by, even, and not knowing if he's guilty . . ."

"Guilty? Guilty of what?"

"Of . . . of . . . oh, Tess, he simply ran away, sneaking out like that before daylight."

"So did Les!"

"Yes, but . . ." I couldn't keep it back any longer. I thought if she was going to have it to face she'd better have it right away so she could meet it and get it over with. "He wrote a letter to Mark Crosby on the train— Gerry did, I mean. He as much as told Mark to get out and

stop sticking his nose in other people's business. He told
him to let sleeping dogs lie."

"Darned good advice, too, if you ask me."

"But, Tess, Mark can't let it lie. That's what he's up
here for."

"Oh," Tess said slowly, lighting a cigarette and watching the smoke while it drifted away. "Is that what he's up
here for? I told you you'd better find out. But I'll bet you
one thing." She sat up suddenly. "I'll bet you, you don't
know who owns the dog."

"No . . ."

"I do."

"Tess, do you know what you're talking about?"

"I sure do. And it's because I know that I think Gerry's
advice is one hundred per cent good. If I were Mark Crosby
and knew where that dog lives—though of course he may
not really know after all—I'd get out quick before it bit me.
It's got hydrophobia," she said, "and I don't mean maybe."

She turned over, digging her elbows into the sand and
resting her chin in her hands. "Look here, Kitty, you're
pretty crazy about that man, aren't you?"

I've always had a perfect mania for blushing. "I don't
know," I said and then I got my chin up. "Yes, I think he's
swell."

"It's all right, honey. And maybe he's all right, too.
Only after what Gerry told me before—before anything
happened about Alicia, your Mark Crosby is barking up the
wrong tree, running around on the wrong leading string—
oh well, you know what I mean. I mean that there's a worm
around here I'd give a good deal to step on right now.
It's your Mark Crosby's Mr. Richmond, and he's the king
worm of the lot—a regular snake in the grass."

Of course, the trouble is I was beginning to agree with
her, but while I didn't really know what Mark thought

about it all I did know he wasn't working blind. Besides, she was getting her metaphors all mixed, the way she does when she gets excited and talking fast.

"Good heavens, Tess! You'd think we lived in a zoo. What did Gerry tell you?"

She began digging in the sand with that shell again, and she wouldn't look at me.

"You wouldn't believe me," she said, "if I told you. Because you think Mr. Richmond's all right just because Mark Crosby's back of him. And you think Gerry is all wrong because of that story about him and Alicia Richmond in school. Oh yes, he told me—he told me yesterday. Told me that was the *story,* but it wasn't the truth. That the truth was something he'd sworn he'd never tell and that Mark Crosby knew it and his precious Mr. Richmond was mixed in it up to the neck. And that if it hadn't been for all that, and Mr. Richmond's insisting on sticking his nose in things up here, there wouldn't have been any of this trouble. But I don't suppose all that will make any difference to you. I suppose you'll keep right on believing Mark Crosby when he tells you that what he's up here for is to get things straightened out."

"Tess! Tess, please . . . I can't help it, can I, if I believe that what Mark is telling me is the truth?"

Tess smiled, a funny, twisted sort of a smile. "No, I don't suppose you can. And I can't help it if I believe that what Gerry tells *me* is the truth. The trouble is, both things *can't* be true. So I suppose you and I are deadlocked."

"Oh Tess, we're not! Please . . . you love Gerry and I . . . I think Mark Crosby is absolutely swell, and I've got a crazy notion that both things are true . . . only . . ."

"Only what?" Tess sounded pretty ironic, and it seemed to me I simply had to make her see what had just struck me.

" . . . only you and I just know part of the truth, and maybe Gerry knows part of the truth and Mark Crosby, too, and if we'd all get together and compare notes, things could be straightened out the way Mark wants them to be."

Tess smiled at me, and if it wasn't a very nice smile I couldn't blame her because I could see that she was trying to be brave and loyal and so she had to be defiant and maybe even nasty, too.

"No thanks. The way I'm feeling right now about Mark Crosby—I'm sorry, Kitty, but it's so—a proposition like that sounds altogether too much like an invitation from the spider to the fly. I just wish they'd get out—both of them—Mr. Richmond and Mark Crosby, too, and let Sidley's Cove go back to being itself again."

"How can it go back? How can it ever be the same after Alicia's dying like that? You know it can't."

"I don't see why not! Dr. Carver says her death was accidental and nobody's to blame, so why on earth . . ."

"Oh! How did you know? I was going to tell you, Tess, so you wouldn't worry any more. About yourself, I mean."

"I'm not worrying about myself, Kitty. I'm worrying about . . . And as for who told me? Who didn't? The whole Cove knows it. Nobody's talking about anything else."

"You're worrying about Gerry, aren't you, Tess?"

"Yes! And I'll keep right on worrying as long as Mark Crosby thinks it's his business to stir things up in Sidley's Cove."

Her head was up and I could see by the way her lips were quivering that she was trying not to cry, and I kept thinking, Tess . . . Tess . . . you're my best friend, don't let's let things hurt us like this. Don't let's believe a thing until we *know!*

"Alicia's dead!" Tess said. "And all the fuss in the world won't bring her back. My dad used to say— whenever Mother'd bring up anything just to talk about it all over again—'Vinny, for heaven's sake, let the dead past bury its dead' and Mother'd shut up and forget about it. That's what everybody at Sidley's Cove ought to do about Alicia—shut up and forget.

"And as far as Gerry's concerned, nothing anybody can do or say—ever—will make me believe he's anything but straight. Nothing he could ever do—not even if he never wrote me or wired me or phoned me or came near me again . . . only he will when Mark Crosby and Mr. Richmond get out of here and stay out—for good . . ."

She had jumped up and was standing there with her hands clenched tight at her sides and the tears streaming down her face, and then all of a sudden she broke off and stood staring down the beach, and took hold of my arm hard and said:

"Look, Kitty—look!"

And I looked where she pointed and I saw two men running across the road from between the trees in front of the Greene place and go down to the dock to where the *Lark* was moored. And one of them was Mark and the other was Mr. Richmond and they got on board and I heard the motor splutter and beat out in that fast, staccato way it had and I heard Mark's voice call out, "O. K." and I saw Fred cast off the ropes from around the mooring piles and the *Lark* started up and pulled away.

And Tess said, "I'm glad! I'm glad! Oh, Kitty, I'm sorry, too . . . I'm sorry about you, but I'm glad."

All I could think was that I knew just how Tess had felt when she said, "Nothing he could ever do would make me think he's anything but straight. Not even if he never wrote me or wired me or phoned me . . ." And I kept holding onto that while I watched the *Lark* grow smaller and smaller, heading out to round the point, leaving a widening white wake behind it in the blue water.

12

It was all very well to stand there on shore when the *Lark* pulled out suddenly like that with Mr. Richmond and Mark on board and Mark's not saying good-by, or telling me he was going to do it, even, and keep my chin up about it. But it was something else again to hang onto feeling the same way while the days dragged out through the week and I didn't hear a word from him.

There must be something, though, to that business about misery's loving company, because Tess and I stuck together like two shipwrecked sailors. That is, until Friday afternoon, when we wandered down to the beach to swim with Ruth, and Arch came along and joined us.

Ruth had kept close to the house and when at last she came out she looked as if she had been crying for a week. She had got hold of herself, though, and even talked about Alicia to Tess and me and said she was sorry she had been such a cat.

"Cat!" Tess sat up quick in that nice, indignant way she has when she gets mad at something she thinks isn't fair. "Who wouldn't have been a cat? I was catty enough, and since we're all going into the confession business I'll admit I'm sorry, too. Only I think now that maybe it wasn't all her fault."

"Why wasn't it? What's so different about her? Why couldn't she be like the rest of us and just . . . just be friendly?"

"I don't know," Tess said, "really. All I know is that she'd had a bad deal. She was lonesome and unsure and afraid. Gerry told me . . ." When she said Gerry's name I could see she knew she was only treading water to keep her head up. But it was up all right and when she went on she sounded a lot more like Tess. "When Gerry told me, it was the afternoon of the day she died and I was mad clear through and wouldn't believe him. I thought he was just stalling, making an excuse for the way he was acting. I don't now. I do believe him now—all the way—and I know it was somebody else's fault and that her father was mixed up in the whole thing!"

"Where does Arch come in?" Ruth said.

"Arch wasn't crazy about her! Honestly, Ruth. At least I don't think he was. It was just that . . . that he thought he ought to make it up to her somehow . . . Oh, Ruth, I don't *know,* I tell you, but you've simply got to forget about all that and not take it out on Arch any longer. Arch is as miserable about it as you can possibly be. I know he is. It's just he's so bull-headed stubborn when he gets his mind set on anything that he forgets everything else except what he's doing. Please, Ruth, you've got to make up!"

"What about the way he insisted on going down on the boat?"

"Well, he didn't go, did he?"

We'd all been being so set on what we were talking about that we didn't see Arch coming along the beach toward us and we didn't even know he was there until he was right beside us, almost, and we heard his voice.

"No, I didn't go, thank God! But it wasn't my own good sense that stopped me."

It was the first time I'd seen Arch really since the day we'd listened in on his father and mother and Mr. Richmond. I'd seen him once or twice from a distance, hanging around the docks where the fishing boats come in, with his canvas, and painting like crazy. And when I saw him now, standing there, looking down at Ruth, I could tell he'd worked it all out of his system and was wanting to take up where he'd left off, if she'd let him. And then it dawned!

"Arch!" I was terribly excited and glad, all of a sudden, and I felt pretty sheepish, too. "That's why Mark Crosby cleared out so fast—to keep you from going along!"

"Of course," Arch said. "What did you think? And to give me time to cool off, too, and see what a fool I'd been making of myself."

"Then he'll be back! He said he'd be gone about a week, so he'll be back . . ." I felt pretty silly now that I saw the whole thing. "Of course! Fred Mack's with them. They'll be back if only to bring Fred."

I saw Tess look at me, quick, but Arch wasn't paying any attention. There was only one person in the world he was interested in right then.

"Ruth . . . can you take it that I'm sorry?"

Ruth just said, "Arch!" and he sat down beside her and took one of her hands and began sifting sand through her fingers, and there were tears in her eyes and she looked awfully happy, but she looked pretty miserable, too, and scared, somehow.

"I've got to tell you something, though, Arch. I've got to tell all of you something before I can stand it for you to be friends with me again."

"O. K." Arch said, "But we're friends, whatever it is."

Ruth held his hand tight for a minute and then drew hers away and looked at all of us with that miserable, frightened look.

"Maybe you won't be, when you know! What on earth do you suppose I've been shutting myself up the way I have and crying and crying, trying to make up my mind . . . trying to get my nerve up to tell?

"I don't know whether they'll do anything to me or not. I don't know what anybody will do, but I can't keep it in any longer. I didn't mean to kill her. Honestly, I didn't mean to kill her. You've got to believe that. I didn't even mean to hurt her, really, I don't think. It's just I was mad clear through and I didn't realize people could die . . ."

She was crying hard, the tears streaming down her face and her face so white and frightened.

"Ruth . . . Ruth, darling . . ." Arch's arm was around her for all he was on the beach and everybody looking. "Ruth, honey, don't talk like that. You didn't kill Alicia. You couldn't have killed Alicia. She fell, that's all. She fell and there was that big rock . . ."

"She didn't fall! She tripped! She tripped over my foot. . . . and there was that rock . . . I was on the end and I was mad and I put my foot out . . . Oh, Arch, you'll never love me again. Nobody . . . none of you . . . What's going to happen to me?"

She was crying so hard everybody on the beach could see it, and Arch stood up and lifted her. "I'm going to take her home," he said. "She's got no business being out here talking like that."

Tess jumped up and went over close and grabbed Ruth's wrists and looked straight into her eyes.

"Pull yourself together! I did. I thought it was my fault, too, but it wasn't. It wasn't anybody's fault, no matter what you think. It was an accident. Do you hear?" Tess was getting pretty hysterical, I thought, as though she was still trying to convince herself, too. "It was an accident! Everybody says it's an accident. Do you hear?"

All the time she had been talking I was thinking, Oh dear, what if Mark knew that? I don't think Ruth did it because I don't think Ruth ever in the world deliberately planned to murder anybody, and Mark said that it was murder, deliberately planned, and that whoever did do it is going to murder other people if he doesn't catch them quick. But to catch them he's got to have all the facts, *all* the facts, *all the facts* . . .

And then Tess saw my face.

"Kitty!" she said. "You'd tell Mark Crosby!"

I felt simply awful, standing there with those people I'd known and liked all my life and with them thinking I was a perfect Judas, and knowing better than I'd ever known anything before that I was right and that when I saw Mark again . . . I'd have to tell him.

"Oh, Tess . . ." I said, and just stood there. I couldn't even move.

Arch was looking at me, too, and Ruth, not saying anything—just looking at me—and all at once I realized, for the first time, what a terrible decision it was the night I made up my mind which side I was on. Because they thought I was being a traitor and I knew I wasn't. If I gave in now I'd be doing it because I was afraid of what my friends would think of me and how they'd act toward me and I knew I mustn't if I thought anything of them at all.

"O. K." Tess said and her face went all hard. I thought Arch looked at me as though he understood, but I wasn't sure, and they turned away and started walking across the beach toward home, leaving me there alone.

It had been hot all day, with the bay like glass, but as I stood there looking out over it, seeing it as I'd seen it every summer since before I could remember, holding my lips tight together to try to keep myself from crying, the wind shifted and began coming in from the east, mean and penetrating. I shivered and thought about Mark, and wondered where he was and what he could be doing. "Keep him safe . . ." I kept saying over and over to myself, "Keep him safe . . ." Because if anything happened to Mark now I didn't see how on earth I could stand it to go on living.

I went back up to the house, and after a while we had dinner and Mother said she and Dad were going over to the Herrods' for bridge and what was I going to do. I said I thought I'd go up and read a while—there was a new book that had come in the afternoon mail. Mother looked at me but I must have kept my face from showing anything, because she just said, "All right. Don't sit up too long. Hurt your eyes . . ." and she and Dad went out and I sat up in my window in the dark where I could look out at the water that was foaming in all along the beach. I kept thinking about what Ruth had said, and then all this business that Gerry had told Tess and that I'd certainly never hear it now, the way they were feeling about me. Nobody would ever tell me anything again, or trust me . . .

I must have fallen asleep there with my head on my arms that were resting on the sill because I didn't see the lights of the *Lark* until after I'd heard the sputter and beat of her motor as she throttled down and I woke up to see her sliding into dock.

I jumped up fast and put a coat around my shoulders because I was chilled clear through with the wind that had been coming in the open window. As I ran downstairs I heard the old mantel clock that's been there since I can remember chime twelve and I knew that the house was empty and that Mother and Dad hadn't come home yet.

When I ran past the Herrods' I saw Les coming around from the back of the house. He was wearing a beach robe and I remember thinking how funny it was of him to be swimming alone so late. I said "Hello," but he didn't answer me and I thought, Oh dear, nobody's going to be speaking to me from now on. Except Mark!

I ran up the road toward the Greene place past where the Herrods' *Felicity* was moored and I held my coat tight around me because the wind cut through the thin lawn of my dress and my footsteps clattered along the planking of the dock and I was frightened and felt terribly alone so that, even before I had reached the boat, I called out, "Mark! Mark, are you there?"

And then I saw him. He was out on the dock making fast the lines and he tightened a knot and turned and saw me, too.

"K-k-kathie!" he said and took my arms in his two hands and held them tight, and I knew he was excited and he looked terribly tired and discouraged, and I'd never seen him like that and I suddenly thought something must be awfully wrong and I said:

"Where's Fred? Where's Fred Mack?"

He couldn't do anything, for a minute, except shake his head, but I knew from the way he looked even before he told me.

"Drowned . . . off Point Betsy . . . this afternoon when the wind turned east. My God, Kathie—this thing's almost got me licked."

13

Naturally, Fred's being drowned like that was pretty much of a shock to the whole place—the village and the Cove, too, and for a while they even talked about calling off the Festival on account of it. But it would have to be the end of the world, really, I guess, to stop the Festival and then Mother talked to Mrs. Mack about it and Mrs. Mack said there was a ship's model in a bottle Fred had been making for them to sell in the Old Timers' booth and that settled it. The model wasn't quite finished but, of course, that wouldn't make any difference about its selling, under the circumstances, and it seemed, somehow, as though Fred was almost saying, "Go ahead. Don't stop on account of me," the way he would have if he'd been alive and been taken sick or something.

You see, the Cove Association Festival is sort of an institution, like Sidley's Cove itself. Nobody knows when it started, I guess, except some of the really old timers like the Greenes who always kept track of everything and maybe people like Fred and Bert Hennebery. It's just that every year, before the season ends, everybody gets together and they have a big party that spreads through all the houses and there are booths on the lawns and at least one orchestra—good years, two—and fireworks and all that. Everything's wide open and the people from Sidley's Cove

and the farmers and their wives and kids and the fishermen—well, everybody—come to it and buy things and pay
for dance tickets.

It's supposed to be to raise funds for fixing up the
beach and keeping the pavilion in repair and things like
that, but I don't think they've made much on it for quite
a while. It's simply that it got started one time a lot of
years back and nobody could stop it if they wanted to and
nobody seems to want to. Specially the village people. So
every year from early August on Mother and Mrs. Conover
and the Herrods and the Willoughbys and the Arnolds and
all the rest of the cottagers who have been there for a gen-
eration or two are up to their necks getting ready for it.
And they call on all the young ones like me to run around
the country for them finishing up odds and ends.

It worked out fine for me because, even though Mother
asked me what on earth was the matter with Tess and me
and wasn't I seeing a great deal of that young man, she was
pretty busy all the time and didn't pay much attention,
really. So after Tess and Ruth turned thumbs down on me
I went just about every place with Mark.

One of the things I had a hard time getting used to in
Mark was the way he usually thought all the things I didn't
think mattered much were terribly important and those
I got excited about he just laughed off. Like when I told
him about Ruth.

"Maybe she tripped Alicia," Mark said, "and maybe she
didn't. It's much the same situation Tess found herself in.
That's the trouble with a mess like this. Everybody who's
ever had a grudge against somebody who dies suddenly—
and tragically—as Alicia did, gets to brooding over it, if
they're pretty decent people, and wondering if, subcon-
sciously, they didn't have something to do with it. From
that to making an actual connection isn't a far step. Ruth

and Tess can both rest easy, though, about the way Alicia fell, because it wasn't a fall she died of."

"Oh," I said, and began to feel as though I could breathe again. "I'll tell them that . . ."

But Mark shook his head. "Not right away, Kathie. Not till we find out—for sure what she *did* die of and who is responsible. Please . . . That is, if you can stand up under being ostracized for just a little longer."

I said of course I could, but sometimes it wasn't easy, particularly when the rumpus began about Fred's death, with Dr. Carver and everybody asking Mark all kinds of questions and Steve Brownlow and Art Stewart getting an investigation going that looked as though it would make a lot of trouble for Mr. Richmond for a while.

Mark went straight to Dr. Carver the day after they docked and told him all he knew, which wasn't much because he hadn't been on deck when Fred Mack fell overboard. And I went along with Mark because Mother had asked me to pick up a Star-of-Bethlehem quilt Mrs. Carver had just finished for the Festival, and anyway Mark said I might as well.

We stopped at Dr. Carver's house first to get that over with and because Mark thought maybe the doctor might drop in home before going on to his office. When Mrs. Carver had called up Mother to tell her the quilt was ready she had said the doctor was back country seeing to the Briggs baby that had come down sick in the night, though for her part she didn't think it was green apples at all, but just that wind.

I don't know whether it's like that in other places along the coast but in Sidley's Cove the whole town is absolutely hipped on the idea that an east wind always brings something bad and every time it blows in, mean and nasty, from the water, they go around with their shoulders hunched up and a weather eye out for trouble. And of course Mrs. Carver always has been the worst of the lot when it comes to any superstition that's going.

I'd known her ever since I was four when she gave me a tiny rag doll with a china head and black, painted hair to make me feel better after Dr. Carver had taken out the dried bean I'd poked up my nose. She was a little woman with a sweet, busy face and she'd been born in Sidley's Cove and he hadn't, coming in from down state somewhere to set up in practice right after he was out of medical college and had had a year in the city.

It kind of bothered the doctor sometimes, I knew, the way she kept picking up new superstitions from all over the countryside. But once in a while something funny happened about one of them and then he was in a spot. Like the time he got warts, himself, and couldn't get rid of them and she told him to steal a piece of salt pork out of Bill Hennebery's pork barrel and rub the warts with it and throw the pork away over his shoulder and not look back. And he did it. Just to show her up, he said. And the warts went away.

Of course she told a lot of people, like Bertha Mack, but the doctor didn't say anything about it himself until one time when Henry Brownlow—Steve's boy—got warts and his mother took him in to Dr. Carver and he told Henry he could try that pork idea if he wanted to, but not to hold *him* responsible. Mrs. Brownlow told my mother and she said he turned red as a beet while he was talking and sort of grumbled, "One of Mary's crazy superstitions . . . wouldn't tell you if your pa wasn't sheriff so he can get you out of trouble if Bill catches you at it."

Anyway, that's Mrs. Carver for you, and Mark and I had no more than knocked on the door when she opened it and said, "I knew that was you, Katherine, because I just put some beans on to soak and when I heard you knocking I said, 'That's Katherine Edwards, sure as shootin' . . .'"

"Mother said you had the quilt ready, Mrs. Carver, and this is Mark Crosby who's been staying with the—with Mr. Richmond. At the Greene place," I said. "He'd like to see Dr. Carver if he's in."

"Why, come in. Come right in, Mr. Crosby. You can wait here for him just as well. Come on in, Katherine." She looked up at the big, black marble clock that stood on the mantel in the parlor—the one I'd listened to more than once when I was little, chiming out the quarter hours. "He'd ought to be back most anytime now. Been gone for almost an hour—out to Briggs's, you know. The baby . . . poor thing, I hope it comes along all right, but with that east wind . . . Dave won't listen to me when I tell him the only thing to keep away summer complaint is a piece of asfedity tied around your neck and if I had any young ones—which I'm sorry to say we never had a sign of— they'd all wear it—doctor or no doctor."

I knew she'd keep right on going like that as long as we were there unless the doctor came in and I thought, good heavens, she'll drive Mark crazy, but his eyes were crinkling at the corners and he was listening to her as if he was really interested, so I kept still. It's just I'd always heard so much of it.

"I had a nurse when I was a kid," he said, "used to keep a piece of asafetida around my neck all the time when I wasn't near my mother. I can remember now how it used to smell . . ."

"And I'll warrant it kept the sickness away from you, didn't it?" Mrs. Carver was tickled pink, leaning forward on the edge of a straight, hard chair, her hands caught together in her lap.

"Well, of course I'm not the one to say, because I was always a husky kid but I got a whale of a stomachache one time when my nurse was out for the afternoon and she swore by all her sainted aunts that I'd have been all right if she hadn't taken the fetty off my neck when she left me, for my mother's sake."

"You would have, too, and I'll warrant if she got home quick enough and put it back on again you got well right off. Didn't you now?"

"That's something," Mark said grinning that wide, nice grin of his, "I'll never know. Because I was rushed off to the hospital and operated on before she had time to get back. Emergency operation—appendicitis."

"Oh!" Mrs. Carver lifted her hands the way she always did when anybody said anything about the doctor. "Well, after all, appendicitis!" And her expression said, perfectly plain, that *that* sort of thing belonged in the doctor's world and was something she wouldn't think of interfering with.

"There's a lot more in charms, though," she went on after a decent minute of respect, "than most people will give credit to. Not that asfedity's a charm, really, but still . . . Take Fred Mack, now. He had one kept him safe—land and sea—for forty years, and if he hadn't forgot and left it home this time he wouldn't be dead now. Bertha says she tried to catch you when you left, but you didn't hear her call and she figured maybe it didn't really matter, any way, so she didn't run after you. She wishes she had, though, now . . ."

It sounded just like all her other talk to me and I thought Mark was taking it the same way I was at first because he didn't move a muscle and his face didn't change at all, but when he stuttered I sat up and listened, too.

"Ch-ch-charm! What k-k-kind of a ch-charm?"

"Land sakes!" Mrs. Carver said, and her sweet face was all pink with concern. "I don't mean to be nosy, Mr. Crosby, and I hope you won't take offense but if you're given to sputtering much, and you'll put three marbles in your mouth—just plain marbles—and practice in front of the mirror with them night and morning for a month . . ."

Mark's face was all twisted up with trying to get things out and I thought, oh dear, I wish she wouldn't and finally he managed to say:

"N-n-not much, Mrs. C-c-carver. J-j-just at all th-the wrong t-t-times when m-m-marbles wouldn't be qu-qu-quite the right th-th-thing. Wh-wh-what *k-k-kind* of a charm?"

You could see Mrs. Carver was feeling pretty bad about the whole thing. She liked Mark, and she felt sorry for him because he stuttered, though she didn't need to. He didn't mind it at all, himself, except when it got in his way and slowed things up like now. But there were almost tears in her voice when she said:

"I do wish I could tell you that, Mr. Crosby. But of course Bertha Mack's never told *me,* being so close-mouthed as she is about things. And anyway, she wouldn't tell me *that.* The surest way to spoil a charm is to let somebody else know what it is. For all I know Fred never told her himself. She just guessed it, I presume, the way a woman will when she's been living with a man for forty years. You take the doctor now, he's never *told* me, right out, but I know he carries . . ."

She stopped because the front door had opened and you could hear Dr. Carver's quick, sure step in the hall.

"Well now," she said, "there's the doctor back and I haven't given you that quilt yet, Katherine. You just wait a minute and I'll bring it right down."

She ran upstairs and you could hear her rummaging around, opening drawers and closing them again and saying, "Oh dear, now wherever *did* I . . . ?" And I kept looking at Dr. Carver and wondering what on earth could be the charm he carried.

14

Dr. Carver, said, "Hello, Katherine. Mr. Crosby, how are you?" and went past us with that brisk, hurrying step of his, into the kitchen. "Be with you in a minute," he called back and you could hear the clatter of china and the sound of a pan being moved across the iron top of the range. He was with us in a minute, too, or not much more, anyway, carrying a cup and saucer and a piece of buttered bread. "Didn't have time for breakfast this morning. Called out a little after five. Mary always keeps the coffee hot for me, though."

"Oh!" I said, "the Briggs baby . . ."

"Pull her through, I think. Hope so. Colic . . ."

He didn't even sit down but just stood there, balancing the bread, between bites, on the edge of his saucer and drinking the steaming coffee.

"Fred Mack's dead," Mark said. "Drowned . . ."

The doctor nodded. "Yes, I know."

"Of course. News travels fast around here, doesn't it?"

"Brownlow phoned me out at Briggs's. Wants to ask everybody a lot of questions."

"Yes. I suppose so."

"Well . . ." The doctor finished his coffee, carried the cup and saucer out to the kitchen, and called, "Mary, I'm going on. If anybody wants me I'll be at the office."

"Now you just hold on a minute, Dave. There's a quilt here Mrs. Edwards wants Katherine to pick up for the Festival, and Bertha Mack brought me over the ship's model poor Fred started before he died, so she might as well take that along while she's about it, too."

Mrs. Carver had the quilt all wrapped up in paper to keep it clean, I guess, and the ship's model was in a box. She started to give them to me but Mark said:

"Here, Kathie, I'll take care of them. You drive."

Mrs. Carver followed us to the door and kept right on talking. "You tell your mother, Katherine, that I was going to take it up to her myself and I ran in to see Bertha a minute and got held up because Bertha couldn't get it out of her head how she wasn't easy in her mind about Fred." Mrs. Carver sighed, standing there with her head on one side like a sad, little bird. "And to think that was only yesterday . . ."

You could tell Dr. Carver wasn't hearing a word she said because he just smiled in an absent-minded sort of way. "That's all right, Mary. We'll be going along now."

"Why wasn't Mrs. Mack easy in her mind about Fred, Mrs. Carver?"

"Because he'd left that charm at home, like I told you."

"Charm!" The doctor just about exploded, and he opened the door and went out and we followed him, but you could hear Mrs. Carver talking all the way down the walk to the street where the cars were parked.

". . . and I feel mighty bad about it now, because I was trying to cheer her up and I said she had no cause to worry because them that was born to be hanged never died on the sea . . ."

On the way to Dr. Carver's office, Mark opened the box that had the ship's model in it and took out the bottle and turned it slowly in his hands.

"It's a beauty!" he said. "Nice old bottle, too. Must have been kicking around the Macks' house for a good many years. Name blown right in—they don't do that much any more."

He was holding it up to the light when I stopped in front of Dr. Carver's office and he put it back in its box and left it in the car with the quilt.

I hadn't been able to get my mind off that charm business Mrs. Carver had been talking so much about and I guess Mark hadn't, either, because when the doctor opened the door and held it for us to go in, Mark smiled at him and said,

"You don't happen to be just a little bit touchy about charms, do you, Doctor, because you have a sneaking fondness for one yourself?"

"Who, me?" He turned around quick, scowling at both of us over the tops of his glasses under his bushy, graying brows. Them he smiled, the funny smile that always made me feel safe, somehow, but not quite sure, either, when I was a little girl, because it made him look as though he was laughing at you and at himself at the same time.

"Hmph!" he said. "Sit down, Crosby. Katherine—you can run along if you want to and take those things to your mother. Mr. Crosby, here, 's got something he'd like to get off his chest from the looks of things."

He had his old pipe out of his pocket and was filling it from a leather pouch he had had from the time I could first remember. When I'd been little the flowers that were painted on it, and the names, hadn't faded much yet and I can still see it in his hands with the "To David—From Mary" showing up bright red against the brown leather when he said, "Measles," and I had to stay in bed for a week and have the shades kept down. And I remember thinking it was funny doctors had first names just like other people and wondering who Mary was. And all of a sudden, somehow, I knew that that was his charm that was supposed to keep him safe and I thought maybe it did, too.

All that had gone through my head fast, the way things do, and I was feeling funny and choked up when I heard Mark say, "Kathie might as well stay, Dr. Carver, if you don't mind. She knows quite a lot about this business. She's . . . helping me out."

Dr. Carver struck a match and drew the flame into the bowl of his pipe in little, sharp puffs, looking at me over it as though he were seeing me for the first time.

"Hmph! Smart girl, Katherine . . . Always was."

He leaned back in the swivel chair with, the worn leather seat that he had had ever since he'd been in practice. He had a roll top desk that was all mussy with the bills he was always meaning to send out and hardly ever did. The medical books he had had when he went through college were lined up, row on row, on the shelves of the sectional bookcases that had glass doors that lifted up and slid in. Their backs were faded and cracked and they didn't look as though he had touched one of them in years. There were some open shelves, though, on the other side of the room stacked with copies of the *Journal* of the A. M. A. and one long row of books with new, clean bindings and bright lettering. I could make out one title that was *Legal Medicine and Toxicology* and another that said *Modern Criminal Investigation* and right beside it a copy of *I Shot the Albatross* with its bright red cover and Mark's name under the title in gold. It made me feel the same way, somehow, as seeing that "To David— From Mary" on the doctor's leather pouch when I was a kid, and I turned around fast and looked hard at the new white sterilizer Dr. Carver had standing on a double electric grill near his desk. I came back with a start, though, to here and now when Dr. Carver said:

"You didn't recover the body. Is that right?"

Mark said, "Right," and Dr. Carver, quick and sharp:

"How'd that happen?"

"I wasn't on deck. Richmond can't swim. And besides, in that water . . ."

"All hearsay, then. Eh?"

"Every bit of it."

"Hm! That's going to be bad—maybe. How soon did you get out there?"

"Soon as I could. Which wasn't very fast. I was up forward at the wheel, taking it over from Fred while he went aft to shift the stuff that was out on deck into the cabin. Wind had picked up suddenly from the east and you could hear the deck chairs banging all over the place. We started rolling plenty and I swung her hard, trying to get her out of the trough. Richmond and Fred clattered down the companionway with the chairs and then Fred went up again, 'to take a look at the weather' Richmond says. He'll tell you himself, so I oughn't to go into it, where he was when he saw Fred go over. All I know is I was having a hell of a time with the wheel and I yelled at Fred to come on forward and give me a hand and Fred yelled back, 'Hold her steady, Mr. Crosby. Hold her where she is,' and right after that Richmond yelling for me bloody murder.

"Everything was making a terrible racket, banging around, and the exhaust cutting way up out of the water. What I know about boats I know from when I was a kid and that's mostly sail. I was never out in a wind like that before with a motor and I made a mess of it, getting myself so she was pitching fit to break her back. I roared out at Richmond, 'For God's sake, what do you want? I can't leave this wheel!' and he came down into the cabin in one jump and he was white as a sheet. You know how God-awful a big, red-faced man like that looks when he goes white, doctor. He just said, 'Crosby . . . Fred's overboard' and

slumped down on the bench beside me and sat there with
his teeth knocking together.

"I suppose he must have realized, even then, that there
wasn't any use—which I didn't—and how the whole thing
would look on shore, but all I could think of was, My
God! You can't supply say a man's overboard and let it go
at that. I pulled him to his feet and shoved him behind the
wheel and said, 'Hang onto it. Just hang onto it' and got
aft as fast as I could."

Mark had been talking hard, leaning forward in his
chair, and when he got to that point he made a helpless
gesture with his hands.

"There wasn't any sign of Fred. Not a sign! I stood
there, looking at that water as though I could look a hole
right down into it wherever Fred was and I thought, Hell
of a deck rail this thing's got, anyway. It'd only be safe on
a pond. And then I thought, My God! I'd better turn her
around. He's been left behind!"

Mark's face looked the way it had the night before—
drawn and tired, only by then he was keyed up and ready
to fight, not beaten and done for.

"Just try it, though," he said, "I told you I don't know
much about motors and there I was in a mean, inshore
wind and the sea piling up heavier every minute and a man
at the wheel who didn't know east from north, even if he
could have handled it, and all that water out there . . . Listen, doctor, there's been too damned much water involved
in all these deaths."

Dr. Carver had been drawing at his pipe, watching
Mark, while he talked, through the cloud of smoke around
his head. He took the pipe out of his mouth and looked at
the stem a minute, the way I remember he always did when
he was thinking hard about something.

"Yes," he said, "water's a great solvent. And, of course,
if you can lose 'em in it . . . Could Fred swim?"

"Haven't the faintest idea. Something to find out. All I know is Richmond said he went down . . . ."

The doctor nodded.

"I think Fred could swim." It was the first time I'd opened my mouth since we came in and they both looked at me as though they'd forgotten I was there, and I suppose they had.

"Wh-what do you m-m-mean, you th-th-think? D-don't you kn-n-now?"

If I hadn't known Mark so well by then I would have thought he was furious because his voice was harsh and clipped and he was absolutely glaring at me. But of course when he stuttered like that I knew he was just excited and it didn't mean a thing really—about me, that is.

"No. He was always teasing me—Fred was—and that's one of the things he'd never tell me. Thought it was funny, I suppose, to keep me guessing. I used to ask him when I was a little girl and he'd say things like, 'I'm a fisherman—not a fish' and, 'Water's to drink—when you can't get anything better.'

"Only just before you left, Mark—that morning—he was swabbing the decks and the water was sloshing all around his feet and I thought, my goodness, what if he slipped when the boat was running and with that low deck rail and all and I asked him again if he could swim. He smiled at me the way he always did when he was teasing and he said, 'Not if I can help it' and I said, 'No, but really . . .' and he said, 'I guess I could paddle a spell if I was put to it—only I'm not aiming to be put to it' and I knew there wasn't any use asking him any more because he had said all he was going to say and had shut up like a clam. Only from the way he looked and—I don't know—just from the way he said it, I think he meant he could swim if he had to. Oh, Dr. Carver, you knew Fred. You know what I mean."

I was almost crying because thinking like that had brought him back terribly clear and I remembered the time I'd talked to him and how good he'd been to me and all.

Dr. Carver looked kind of funny around the eyes himself. "Yes, I knew Fred," he said, and then, "What do you make of it, Crosby?"

"What I make of it is that if he could swim, he didn't. Unless Richmond's lying straight through, because he said Fred went down like a plummet and came up again just once. Didn't even yell."

"Hm!" Dr. Carver said. "Yes, I suppose so . . . ."

He cut off short. "There's Stewart and the sheriff."

The street door had opened down below and you could hear the heavy tramp of men's feet coming up the flight of wooden stairs and Steve Brownlow's voice booming out,

"Well, *he's* here, anyway . . . there's that fancy, yellow car."

15

Of course I've known Steve Brownlow just, about all my life, summers, the way I've known most of the people around Sidley's Cove, but I'd never taken him very seriously. Being sheriff, it was his business, for a long time, to keep an eye on the cottages during the winter when they were shut up, and I knew my Dad had said that that was all very well but if you lined up a good caretaker and had him made deputy he'd noticed that things seemed to weather through a whole lot better. So, after the Herrods' boat house was broken into and some motor parts taken by a bunch of boys one winter, the Association had Fred Mack made deputy and nothing much happened after that. Then, too, they started up the State Police about the time Steve was elected for his first term and it didn't seem to me he had anything to do at all except hang around Johnson's Undertaking Parlors waiting for Ed and some of the others to show up so they could get some poker going in the back room. What I mean is, he was easygoing.

Art Stewart was different, though. In the first place he wasn't a Sidley's Cove man. He came from Carworth, inland a ways, and didn't even show up in Sidley's Cove much until he started campaigning for Prosecutor. He had gone into office in the last election and he was young and pretty ambitious, I guess, for around there. Anyway, he had a hard, hot look in his eyes, and when he could get anybody in a corner he liked to shoot questions at them as though he had a gun in his hand.

They both looked kind of funny, though, when Steve opened the doctor's office door and they saw me sitting there. After all, they've known my family for a long time.

"H'are you, doctor?" Steve said. "Morning, Mr. Crosby . . . Miss Edwards. Been looking for you, Crosby." Art Stewart was never a man to beat about the bush. "Richmond, too. Couldn't find him. Not home, anyway."

"You'd find him over at Macks' house." Mark's voice had a little edge to it. He hates cock-and-bull people and I could see right then that he and the prosecutor were going to town. "Went over after breakfast to talk to Mrs. Mack."

"Oh, he did, did he? Bad conscience?"

"What would he have a bad conscience about?"

"Oh, come along out of it, Crosby. Fred Mack's dead, isn't he?"

"Yes, and that leaves Mrs. Mack a widow. Richmond would like to make some compensation—provide for her . . ."

"Mighty fine woman, Mrs. Mack." It was the first thing Steve had said since he had said hello and I could see, in his soft, easy-going, kind sort of face, that he wanted to keep things from coming to trouble if he could. But not Art Stewart.

"And how come she's a widow? How did it happen, Crosby?"

"Mr. Richmond will have to tell you that. I wasn't on deck when it happened."

"Yeah, but he told you, didn't he?"

"Sure. Only you're not going to get any hearsay evidence out of me."

"No-o? Well, I'll tell you one thing, Crosby, and that is we're going to get more evidence out of you or out of somebody than we did on the thing last week. Pretty smooth, weren't you, high-pressuring us into calling it 'accidental' so fast?"

"I didn't hear you kick. You had Dr. Carver's findings."

"Yeah, Dr. Carver's findings without a post mortem. He's coroner. It's up to him."

"Now, Art," Steve was beginning to look worried.

"Dr. Carver's been coroner a long time. There's nobody doesn't listen to what he says."

"Yes, and that's just the kind . . ."

Dr. Carver cleared his throat. He's got a pair of pretty sharp eyes himself, and I've seen him angry a few times in my life and I haven't liked it.

"If you want to bring a malfeasance charge against me, Stewart, go ahead. But until you have, keep a civil tongue in your head. I've seen new brooms before . . . On the evidence and my examination I had to bring in 'accidental' on Alicia Richmond's death. There wasn't anything more to go on. Get an exhumation order if you've got any additional evidence and I'll cut her up."

I felt sick, all of a sudden, hearing them talk like that as though Alicia had been just a body and not a person at all, but I held onto myself tight because I didn't want Mark to think I couldn't take it and make me go home. I wanted to hear everything I could and I'd seen Art Stewart look at me a couple of times as though he wondered what on earth business I had there and I thought any minute he would say something about it and then maybe I'd have to leave.

"I'll cut her up," Dr. Carver said, "but I'm willing to stake forty years of practice against my chances of finding anything I didn't find without it. I knew pretty well what I was up against the minute I heard she was dead and from what Crosby here—and he's a damned sight smarter than any of us when it comes to things like that—had to tell me about the symptoms when she died. You can take it from an old man, Stewart, there's some things a dead body can't often tell you very much about—some kinds of death that don't talk above a whisper, if they talk at all. And your best chance of finding anything out is to hush things up fast and pretend you're not on the trail."

Art Stewart's head had been going down and he was looking like a bull that's getting ready to charge.

"So now you're saying it's murder, are you, Doc? You're talking out of the other side of your mouth. I thought you were the man . . ."

The doctor puffed at his pipe, but it had gone out and he looked around for a match and struck it and drew the flame into the bowl. I thought he would be terribly angry, somehow, at the way Art Stewart was talking to him, but his eyes were laughing and when he started to talk again, he drawled in a slow, dry sort of way.

"If you'll think back on what I just said, Stewart, and you're worth your salt as a prosecutor, you'll find I said no such thing. And if you *are* worth your salt as a prosecutor and you really want to run down crime, you'll play ball with me and with Mark Crosby. That's what he's up here for."

"What in hell *is* he up here for?" Stewart was so mad now he was almost bellowing. "What's he sticking his nose in other people's business for? It's about time Brownlow and me—Steve was just saying the other day—it's about time we knew."

"Oh now, Art, I was only talking. I didn't mean to make any trouble out of it." Steve shuffled his feet and looked so unhappy I couldn't help thinking, My goodness! what did he ever get himself elected sheriff for? He belongs in the grocery business.

All the time there was a funny look on Mark's face. I could, see he was making up his mind about something and at last he said:

"Tell you what, Stewart, I'll make a bargain with you. If I tell you what I'm up here for will you promise to keep *your* nose out of it?"

I'll say this for Art Stewart, and Mark says so too, that he can't be scared out of doing what he starts out to do or bribed, either, and once he's got his teeth in something he won't let go. He just stood there with his hands in his pockets and his head down and he said:

"No! Not if it's my business, too."

There was that nice smile on Mark's long face. "O. K." he said. "Then the battle's on. But you'll have to go back a long way if you want to make my business yours and I'm only going to give you one handicap. I'll tell you that I came up here in the first place about a death that happened twenty-five years ago. And I'm convinced that the two that hit this last week are follow-ups. I think they connect."

I said, "Oh!" I couldn't help it, and Art Stewart looked at me and said, "What's she doing here? She's got no business . . ."

"Yes she has. She's my . . . assistant."

"Assistant, me eye. That's Katherine Edwards and she's right in with the crowd that . . ."

"The better to see them with."

"Traitor to her class—eh?"

"No," Mark said slowly. "Eyes and ears for them to help me find out who is the traitor. Lay off, Stewart. I've told you she's my assistant and if you want to talk to me you can do it with Kathie around."

"Oh, so it's 'Kathie,' is it? Well, in that case . . ." Art grinned and with a lot of people it would have made me mad but, somehow, there wasn't anything really nasty about it. It was just human. The first human thing he had done so far.

"Mr. Stewart," I said, "you've got to believe me. Honestly, I'm all on your side."

"O. K." He didn't look as though he was quite sure but thought maybe he'd better make the best of it. For now, anyway. "What about this twenty-five-year-old murder you've got up your sleeve?"

"That's better! Does either one of you happen to re-member . . . maybe you wouldn't, Stewart, because you weren't a Sidley's Cove boy, but Brownlow ought to . . . about a resorter—a woman—who was drowned twenty-five years ago this summer out there in Sidley's Bay?"

Art Stewart shook his, head, scowling as though he sus-pected Mark was trying to put something over on him. He looked at Steve. Steve was rubbing his chin and then, all of a sudden, he came to life.

"Sure," he said. "I remember. I was pretty much of a kid then—around nine or so, and I remember all the fuss about her going overboard and the Festival's being called off right in the middle. There was some more talk, too, but I can't seem to think up what that was. Only that they dragged—kept, dragging for damned near a week but they didn't find the body. That right?"

"Right. But you don't remember who it was, do you?"

"No. Can't say I do. A boy doesn't pay much attention to stuff like that unless he's connected with the folks."

"The woman who was drowned was Alicia Richmond's mother. Alicia wasn't a year old."

That made me say, "Oh!" too, but nobody paid any attention to me this time.

"How did it happen?" Art Stewart certainly was right there when it came to going after facts.

"Mrs. Richmond was out on the fishing schooner Fred Mack had then, watching the Festival fireworks from the water. She fell overboard."

"Drowned?"

"Your guess on that is as good as anybody's. 'Drowned' is what they had to call it. What everybody thought, in fact—even Mr. Richmond until not long ago. Fred was anchored over the eighty-foot drop-off and an east wind blew up in the night. That and the tide took care of it, perhaps. Or maybe she's still there . . ."

I shivered. I couldn't help it, thinking about Alicia's mother out there eighty feet down or washed out to sea, maybe—dead twenty-five years.

"Out on the boat with Mack?" Art Stewart's eyes were hard and bright and shrewd. "Mack must have been under forty then and he was a fine looking sort of a man. Mr. Richmond wouldn't have been waiting all these years to get even about anything would he? Nothing like that?"

"That would be a fine, tight theory, Stewart, if it didn't have as many holes as a sieve. In the first place, Mrs. Richmond wasn't alone on that boat with Fred. There were a dozen or more other people on board and they all testified at the time—every one of them—that she was perched up on the deck rail so she could see better and lost her balance and fell in. Simple as that. Of course, some of them could have been lying . . . Anyway, she wasn't very strong and she couldn't swim. She went down fast—just the way Fred did. They all testified to it—Richmond and Mrs. Herrod—she'd been Henrietta Greene until that June—and the Willoughbys—Mrs. Willoughby was a bride, too—and the Greenes and their son, Henrietta's brother—he's been dead a couple of years now—and Mr. Conover—he hadn't married Vinny Barnes then. Kathie, here, wasn't born then, either, but her folks were on board. They all told the same story. So you can see that any little, romantic notion about Fred Mack doesn't quite make sense. In the second place, how about Alicia's death this summer? The two—on a Fred Mack theory—don't fit."

Nobody said anything, and Dr. Carver cleared his throat and knocked his pipe out against the heel of his shoe.

"Mr. Richmond," Mark went on, "was hit hard all around. He hadn't been particularly popular with the summer crowd to begin with and he was left a widower with a baby girl who wasn't a year old. Added to that some nasty talk got going. He never knew where it started—whether it was in the village and spread to the cottagers or the other way around. Anyway, the gist of it was that he wasn't Alicia's father."

"Well, was he?" Stewart, after facts, took it all in his stride.

"That's the fun," Mark said, "a particularly venomous type of human being gets out of smearing scandal of that sort. It not only hurts the victim through what other people say and think about him, but it fills his own heart and mind with a gnawing doubt. It's slow poison."

"Ye-es," Stewart said thoughtfully. "And it might make 'em do things they wouldn't do otherwise." His eyes were sharp and he kept watching Mark. "Did Richmond tell you all this himself? Because maybe—it's possible, you know—all this talk didn't get going *after* his wife was drowned but *before*. See what I mean? Maybe he asked her about it, straight out, and she didn't answer him so straight, or even if she did . . . get me? . . . he got to stewing about it and then that night maybe she was extra friendly with somebody in the crowd and he . . . he might of been standing right close to her when he was arguing and . . . and then it ate away at him all. those years about how maybe the girl wasn't his, and so he finally killed her, too . . . ."

"How does Fred Mack's death fit in that picture? What would he kill Fred for?"

"That's easy. Hell of a detective you are! It's plain as the nose on your face. Fred probably suspected him all along—maybe even kind of thought he saw him do it, but wasn't sure. Then when the girl died he speaks his mind and Richmond shoves him off to keep from being found out. People get desperate, sometimes, and pull just one too many and that's the one that trips 'em up."

I'd been listening to Art Stewart, simply fascinated, because the way he told it was so reasonable it sounded as though it might be true. And then when Mark nodded, frowning the way he did when he was thinking hard, I thought, my goodness! Mark thinks it's Mr. Richmond, too.

"That's a tight story, Stewart—fairly tight. But what are you going to do with the fact that Richmond called me in, twenty-five years after his wife's death to get on the trail of her murderer?"

"Twenty-five years after her death!" Stewart certainly sounded triumphant. "And just before his daughter—if she was his daughter—died mighty sudden as well." You could tell he was feeling pretty smart. "By any chance there wasn't anybody on his trail, was there, along about the time he called you in? Nobody'd caught up with him with some information they'd got, had they? It couldn't be, could it, Mr. Crosby, that he got hold of you *before* he killed this—this daughter of his—so he'd have you to hide behind?"

"Yes," Mark said, "it could. Of course. This is a crazy world and anything's possible in it. And somebody did get on his trail. But the way they got on it doesn't fit in very well with your story. You see, Alicia hadn't been very happy for—oh, several years—not since something pretty upsetting had happened to her when she was barely out of school. And Richmond was looking around for a summer place where she could start all over again—make new friends." Mark's laugh was short and a little ironic.

"The trouble with Richmond is, he's bull-headed. When he gets mad, he's mad all through and he forgets everything else in going after what he wants to fight. If he'd had any sense at all he'd never have come up here when he found out that that's where it was.

"You see, he happened to run across a blind ad in one of the Sunday papers that interested him. Described just the sort of place he thought he'd like—which, considering he had a lot of memories about Sidley's Cove, isn't so strange. He'd fought shy of it, though, like the plague, for a quarter of a century—ever since his wife's death and all the trouble that followed it, and he would have kept on fighting shy of it when he found out it was the old Greene place up here if Mr. Greene hadn't received a letter, a day or two after Richmond went in to see him, warning him not to sell or lease to Charles Richmond if Richmond didn't want more trouble of the same kind."

"Well, I'll be . . . damned!" Art Stewart said. "I always did say you never know what these resorters are up to—underneath. But he didn't pay any attention to it—eh?"

"The trouble is, he paid too much attention to it. It was like waving a red flag at a bull. Once he'd got the idea that some person—some one individual and not just fate—had caused him all his trouble—he couldn't think of anything but wanting to run 'em down and fight."

"Who wrote the letter?" Stewart said. "Where'd it come from? Ever find that out, Crosby? Seems to me if you found that out, you'd have the whole thing in a nutshell."

Art Stewart had been roaring so he couldn't hear anything but his own voice, but I'd heard the downstairs door open a minute before and then steps coming up, slow and heavy, as though the person who was walking was terribly tired. The office door opened and Mr. Richmond was standing there with his hand on the knob. His face, that had been all round and smooth only a week before, was full of lines, and his eyes looked like holes somebody had burned in a mask.

He closed the door carefully behind him and walked across the room like a man walking in his sleep, not seeing anything, really, but some horrible dream, and sat down, all slumped over in a chair.

16

Nobody said a word for, anyway, a minute. We just sat there watching Mr. Richmond who was having a terribly hard time getting his breath.

"Stairs . . ." he said, and tried to smile, and then, "Sorry . . . couldn't help overhearing. That letter . . . you tell 'em, Crosby."

"The letter," Mark said, "was postmarked Thornton and of course a lot of people drive over there for one reason or another. Couldn't trace it from that. The handwriting, though, even if it was disguised . . ."

Dr. Carver had been watching Mr. Richmond who reached in his pocket just then, for a cigar. He bit off the end. He slumped down, his hands shaking violently.

"What's the matter, Richmond? Heart?" said Dr. Carver pretty sharply.

Well, maybe it was heart, I thought, but I couldn't help remembering how the night Alicia died I had said, "She's afraid! She's afraid!" when I saw her face in the light just before she fell. Because he looked afraid even while he seemed to be trying to clear his mind and get hold of himself.

"Just about got me," he said. "Can't stand up under this sort of thing forever. Fighting ghosts . . ."

Dr. Carver went over and felt his pulse and then got out his stethoscope and put the ends in his ears and the mouthpiece thing to Mr. Richmond's chest, under his shirt.

"Eat a lot, Richmond? Smoke a lot? Drink pretty regularly?"

"It isn't drinking. What I need's a drink right now."

"No, you don't. What you need is a little moderation. I'm not saying you drink a lot at a time, very often, but I'll bet you do drink pretty regularly. One or two before dinner every night, say, sometimes pile 'em up in the evening if you're with a crowd, never go to bed without at least one Scotch and soda. Am I right?"

"Yes. But that's not it. I tell you I'm O. K.—physically. It's just the strain . . . Enough to make any man seedy. Losing Alicia. . . . Then, this business about Fred right on top of it. Feeling you've got enemies, all around you, managing to keep themselves hidden. My God! It's like fighting ghosts." His tongue moved out to moisten his dry lips. "That business last night . . ."

"What about Fred?" Art Stewart was right in there. "Like to ask you a few questions about Fred, Mr. Richmond."

Dr. Carver had been fussing around in his instrument case ever since he'd finished listening to Mr. Richmond's heart, and he looked up from it at Art Stewart the way a father would look at a bad boy.

"Hold on there a minute, Stewart. Keep your questions to yourself until I tell you it's all right to go ahead or you'll be firing 'em at somebody who's past answering. This man's in bad shape."

He took a hypo out of his bag and filled it in the quick, sure way I could remember he always did things when I was a kid, and rolled up Mr. Richmond's sleeve and shot it in.

"There! Now, for God's sake Stewart, let him catch his breath."

The color came back into Mr. Richmond's face and his breathing that had been shallow and hard grew deeper and a little easier.

"Look here," Dr. Carver said, "I'm going to talk to you like a Dutch uncle, Richmond. You've got to go slow or take the consequences. You could stand all the drinking you do and the smoking and the heavy eating so long as there wasn't any strain. But the minute you had an extra load to carry in the way of worry, your body went on strike. Asthmatic—that's what you've made yourself. For the time being it looks as though you couldn't eliminate the worry but if you don't cut down on the other things you're going to finish yourself off."

"O. K." Mr. Richmond's voice was tired, but he didn't really sound resigned—not to me. "What does that mean? No liquor at all? No cigars? Milk diet? Might as well be dead and have it over."

"Stuff and nonsense! Once you get used to it you'll feel so much better you'll be glad you did it. Yes, you've got to cut 'em all out—for the time being, anyway. That is, if you want to keep yourself in shape to deal with that fine ghost of yours."

"I could deal with it," Mr. Richmond said, "if I could lay my hands on it. It gets away . . ."

"Hmph! What gets away?"

"The ghost . . ." His voice trailed off as though he didn't have the strength—or maybe the will—to say any more.

"Go on!" Mark cut in. "Give it to 'em."

You could see the effort Mr. Richmond had to make to pull himself together but he did it all right.

"Last night," he said, "it was pretty late, when we docked. Crosby here says it was nearly midnight."

"It *was* midnight," I said and then I felt myself blushing in the silly way I do because I knew they'd wonder how I was so sure. "I ran down when the boat docked to see if Mark . . . to see if everything was all right. And the mantel clock chimed twelve as I went through our living room."

"O. K." Art Stewart sounded impatient. "That seems to fix the time all right. What happened?"

"Crosby helped me make fast and then he went on ahead of me—to take Katherine, here, back home. I called after him that I'd lock up and be waiting for him at the house. Of course we were both pretty hard hit by all that business about Fred and just about knocked out by the fight we'd had to put up out there in open water and I don't suppose I was any too level-headed, but habit's habit and I've never left the boat since I've owned her without locking the cabin doors—not unless Fred was on board. I know I locked 'em last night— remember putting the keys in my pocket after I'd seen everything was in order and turned out the cabin lights.

"I went up to the house and let myself in and looked around. Then I made for the kitchen to mix myself a good stiff one and get one ready for Crosby."

"Hm!" Dr. Carver said. "Just as I thought."

Mr. Richmond didn't pay any attention to him. He was staring straight ahead at the wall as though he was seeing things right through it.

"It may have been fifteen-twenty minutes I fussed around. Stands to reason it wasn't much longer than that. I came back into the living room and sat down in the dark over by the window and sipped my drink while I waited. Thinking about Alicia and how empty and lonesome that big house was now she was gone and wondering what I was going to do with myself the rest of my life . . . you know . . .

"About half finished my glass when I noticed lights shining out through the cabin windows of the *Lark*. Crosby must have gone back for something, I thought, and figured they'd go out in a minute and he'd be up. Then I remembered he didn't have a key. I got up at that and stared down there at the boat and I knew the cabin lights weren't on. It was a dimmer light—white and moving . . ."

He was breathing quick and shallow again and looking simply awful. Dr. Carver lifted his hand as though he meant to stop him but Mr. Richmond acted as though he didn't see the hand or anything else much in the room either.

"For a minute I couldn't move . . . you don't know . . . it was like being turned to stone . . . I'd locked that cabin with my own hands! I got hold of myself and went to open the front door. When I couldn't I lost my head and beat it and kicked at it. Then I had sense enough for think what was the matter. Both doors over there have the kind of double lock, you have to turn while you turn the knob unless the catch is fixed. When I'm home it usually is, but of course I'd left things locked up when I left and when I'd come up from the boat I'd been in a hurry and slammed the door after me. I got it open after that, of course, in half a minute but by the time I started running across the lawn toward the boat there weren't any lights in the cabin any longer—they'd gone out."

"What did you find?" Art Stewart snapped. "Boat broken into, was it? Anything gone?"

"Nothing . . ." Mr. Richmond was breathing terribly hard so the sound of it seemed to fill that little room. "All locked up . . . the way I left her . . . nothing . . ."

"Sure you didn't . . . dream it?" It was the way Art Stewart paused when he said that that made it so nasty.

But Mr. Richmond didn't even seem to notice. "No, it wasn't a dream. Crosby saw it, too."

"Oh he did, did he?"

Mark was looking pretty grim around the mouth and I kept thinking, look out, Mr. Stewart, look out!

"Yes," Mark said, "I saw the lights all right. Saw them go out, too, and heard the cabin door slam shut."

"Hear anything else? See anything?"

"Yes, I saw something—somebody—very faint in the beam of the riding light—slide down off the dock into the water."

"Chase 'em?"

"Sure," Mark said, "by taking off into eighty feet of black water and swimming around in circles. It's just the thing I'd do. Do you happen to remember, Stewart, that there wasn't any moon? Or were you asleep at midnight?"

"Moon or no moon, Crosby, you're making a fine job of this business—letting somebody who got on that boat of Richmond's get away like that. Listen here—you say you didn't have any keys to that boat. Who did?"

"Stewart," Mark said—and I thought, here it comes— "I'm not much of a publicity hound—like to let my reputation build itself. Pretty good reputation, though. It hasn't often been questioned by the law or anybody else—at least not for long. Strangely enough, too, my business seems to run to the supernatural. The last time a local officer tried to stir up trouble for me was in a case in Westchester where a man died at sight of his dead grandmother. Hunted that grandmother for six months—and found her. Perhaps you remember . . ."

The way Art Stewart's face changed was positively funny. From looking belligerent and important and all that, it grew almost wide-eyed, like a little boy's when he gets a chance to shake hands with Santa Claus for the first time.

"Hell! Not the Carmody case? Whyn't you say so to begin with? I thought you were just some two-by-four that had a notion he knew more'n men who were right in the game. Well, well . . . the Carmody case . . . why, I remember reading all about that—every word I could get my hands on. Look, I want to ask you some time . . . Brownlow, you remember the Carmody case?"

Steve Brownlow hadn't said a word in ten minutes, it seemed to me, and he just looked absent-minded and sort of goofy, I thought, when he said, "Yes . . . yes . . . I remember . . ."

"Fine!" Mark said, and you could see he was pretty pleased with himself for all he wasn't a publicity hound. "Then I can count on you to work with me from now on, Stewart. That right?"

"You sure can. Why, I remember . . ."

"O. K. Now, let's get down to brass tacks. I didn't follow the person who slid down off the rocks last night because, in the first place it would have been pretty futile and in the second place I didn't want 'em to know they were seen. Anybody thinks he's been seen up to something, he gets cagey. On the other hand, if he thinks he's got away with it, it makes him cocky and he's likely to get careless—play right into your hands."

"Enough rope!" Stewart said, all solemn and important. "That's what I say, Mr. Crosby, just give 'em enough rope and they'll hang themselves."

My goodness, I couldn't help thinking, the Carmody case must have been *something*.

"Yes, or somebody else. But there was still another reason why I didn't follow that person last night. Because I didn't need to. I knew who it was. Knew who it had to be to fit into the picture things've been building for quite a while. It was Les Herrod!"

"Oh, good Lord!" Mr. Richmond groaned.

Art Stewart said, "How do you know, Mr. Crosby? Could you tell me that? How do you know?"

Mark shook his head. "If it's all the same to you, Stewart, I'd rather not—just yet. You see, the one thing a private detective's any good for is to keep things private while he's hunting out trouble. Things about people's private lives that might just as well—or better—be kept private if you can keep 'em that way and still serve justice," he smiled, "and the law. I'm following a private line of investigation—working counterbalances against each other—and it'll be swell of you if you'll let me go ahead for just about a day longer, on my own. Things have got to work fast now, or my game's up. And if it fails I'll be the first to admit it to you and ask you for God's sake to go ahead with everything wide open. O. K.?"

"O. K." Stewart said, but it seemed to me he didn't like that part of it very well. Working *with* Mark Crosby was one thing and standing by and not doing anything while *he* worked was something else again for an ambitious man like Art Stewart.

"I'll give you something to get your teeth into, though. You asked me who had keys to Richmond's boat, and I'll answer you, fair and square. There were three sets. Mr. Richmond always carries one. Fred Mack had another. They were in his pocket when he went down. Alicia Richmond carried the third. That last set—Alicia's—has been missing since the night she died. So has the purse she carried them in."

"Oh," I said. "The one Helen picked up?"

Mark didn't have a chance to answer because Steve Brownlow, who had been just sitting there as though he was in a trance, staring at Mr. Richmond in the funniest way as if he wasn't really seeing him but seeing *through* him, somehow practically roared out:

"My God! I've got it! I remember now. That woman that was drowned—that resorter—she was Mrs. Willoughby's sister. And her husband—Mr. Richmond, there . . . Mr. Richmond, aren't you Bertha Mack's sister's boy from over near Thornton?"

Mark groaned. "Charlie, that leaves your private life about as private as a goldfish."

Mr. Richmond had been sitting with his head sunk down in his hands, and when he lifted his face to look at Steve it was simply terrible.

"Yes," he said, "yes, you're right, Brownlow. And it's all right with me. Only to them it was something I couldn't ever live down—the Willoughbys, I mean. That's where the trouble all started. That's why they've fought me—from the first. Why Crosby and I are both sure Willoughby wrote that letter."

17

Dr. Carver cleared us all out of his office so fast, you'd think we were poison or something.

"Look here," he said, "you people—and that means Steve and Art, too—have got to let this man alone for a day or two. That is, if you don't want his to be the third death this summer. I don't care if he's a Mack or a Willoughby or who he is. As far as I'm concerned, he's a patient, and I'm ordering rest and quiet for him—and a little peace."

Mark drew him to one side and they talked for a minute or two, the doctor nodding every once in a while. When they got through, Mark said he was going to stay with Mr. Richmond while Dr. Carver gave him some additional treatment and then he'd drive him home and put him to bed. Would I take the Fiat and meet him at the Richmonds' dock in about an hour? And if I ran across anybody who'd be willing to do a little nursing for a few days . . .

I said of course, but it was a whole lot easier said than done—meeting him, I mean—because the Festival was supposed to start at eight and Mother wouldn't let me get away with not running errands for her. Which got pretty grim because of some of the places I had to go.

Besides, I had to drive past the store on the way home, and Bill Hennebery was out in front giving somebody some gas.

"Hi! Kitty!" he called and I stopped.

"Your Ma's looking all over hell an' gone for you. You'd better beat it on home. Up to her eyes, she says, in last minute stuff on the Festival and not a soul helping her."

He smiled when he said it because everybody knows the way Mother gets when she's excited and has a lot to do, and he thought, just the way I did, that everybody she could lay her hands on was helping. The people who'd been getting gas drove on and I don't know why except I just wanted to see how he'd take it, but I said:

"Mr. Richmond's sick. He's at Dr. Carver's office and they're taking him home."

"Is that so?" Bill said. He looked kind of funny, I thought. "Too bad . . . nice fellow."

"Listen, Bill." I couldn't help it. I had to know. "Do you know who Mr. Richmond is, about his wife and . . . all that?"

"Yes," Bill said, "sure. Everybody does—us older ones, anyway. Couldn't mistake him in a million years, for all he's changed a lot. Nice boy, he was. Shame he had to get mixed up with that crowd and then walking off with her the way he did . . ."

"Bill," I said, "do you think his wife was murdered?"

Bill shut his lips in a thin line and didn't say anything for a minute. He kept eyeing me in the suspicious way he used to when I was little and said my mother had sent me down for a nickel's worth of candy and he wasn't sure she'd told me I could.

"I'm not saying I do and I'm not saying I don't." He began winding up the gas pump handle so the pump would be ready for the next customer. "All I'm saying is I managed to keep from being mixed up in it then and I'm not aiming to get mixed up in it now."

"But, Bill . . . there's so many people . . . the way Alicia died, too, and then Fred and now Mr. Richmond sick.

If anybody knows anything it seems to me they ought to *tell*."

"There's plenty knows it besides me," Bill said, "if you can get 'em to open up. You or that young man o' yours." He grinned, because of course that made me blush. "I'm not saying there's not things about that whole set-up that your Mr. Crosby mightn't find useful to know. Things a few people I could name—if I was a mind to—aren't too proud of. We're all mighty close-mouthed here in Sidley's Cove and I don't crave to put my neck out—not with things going on the way they are. Besides, I'm not concerned in it—not what you'd rightly call concerned."

A couple of kids were coming up the store steps, after ice cream cones, probably, and Bill set his thin old lips very firm.

"That's all I got to say." He turned around and stomped off into the store and I drove on down to our house and asked Mother what she wanted me to do.

"My goodness, child!" She sat down in a wicker chair that was absolutely surrounded with ground pine and florists' wire and stone crocks and baskets. "I'm just about out of my mind. Here I've got all the decoration to do and everything—absolutely everything, has to be ready by eight. Of course your father's helping me but you . . . No! I'll tell you what you can do—you've got that young man's car again, haven't you? Well, that's a help. First you go on over to Conovers' and ask Vinny to let you have every single crock she's got—we'll have to put the flowers in water right away. And then Edith Willoughby. Run along now, dear, and hurry, please. And if you see Tess and Helen or Ruth . . . or Arch . . ."

I ran down our porch steps thinking, oh my goodness, I might have known it. I couldn't possibly get by, of course, through the whole Festival, with just not having anything to do with any of the people who were so down on me and now I was in for it. I kept wishing and wishing some miracle would clear things up before the Festival itself because I didn't see how on earth I could stand going to it with about half the people I'd called my friends not speaking to me. Oh Mark, I thought, if I didn't trust you so much, if I wasn't sure you know what you are doing . . .

I turned the Fiat into the gravel drive at the Conovers' and got out half hoping I wouldn't run into Tess and hoping I would, too, because I thought if I could only talk to her a minute I'd tell her what had happened since—how Mr. Richmond was sick now,—and she'd have to see Mark was all right and maybe the nastiness, with her, would be over.

She wasn't there, though, and I went through the house looking for Mrs. Conover. She was in the kitchen with their Anna, and both of them were working for dear life making pastes and things for hors d'oeuvres.

"Tess isn't here, dear," she said without half looking up. "And what on earth she's up to I'm sure I don't know. I simply haven't laid eyes on her for over an hour. Of all times . . . I don't think anybody can blame me for being just a *little* provoked . . . After all the Festival *is* the Festival. Two orchestras this year!"

Mrs. Conover is so terribly nice-looking and alive— she's a lot like Tess—and I've always thought it was a shame Mr. Conover died so young even though he did leave her pretty well off, and I'd sometimes wondered why she hadn't married again.

When she said, "Two orchestras!" she whirled, dancing, around the kitchen, holding a jar of anchovies in one hand and laughing and I thought about how well she and Mr. Richmond had been getting along when all the trouble began and how it was simply too darned bad and then what Dr. Carver had said about if I happened to run across somebody who'd be a good nurse . . .

"Mr. Richmond's sick," I said.

She stopped dancing and her black eyes looked terribly big, all of a sudden, and she put the jar of anchovies down on the table and started washing her hands under running water in the sink. I was so tickled I could have hugged her.

"I'll go right over," she said and I couldn't help thinking about how Mother had said, "Vinny never was very conventional" and I thought how swell it was.

"There ought to be somebody in the house with him besides just a maid. Poor man, poor dear . . . and his daughter's funeral hardly over . . . no wonder."

She dried her hands and ran out through the living room and I called after her about the stone crocks, but she didn't even hear me and I had to get Anna to help me find what we could and I kept thinking I hadn't helped Mother much, maybe, by taking Mrs. Conover away from getting the hors d'oeuvres done, but I was glad I'd done it anyway, because she was about the only one except Mother who didn't have a grudge against Mr. Richmond and that, alone, would probably do him good.

I had to go to the Willoughbys' after that and I felt awfully funny about it, knowing what I did and then, just to make it worse, there wasn't a soul around except Mr. Willoughby himself. I had to go clear out to the tool shed, even to find him. That's where everybody keeps crocks and big jars and baskets and things like that for flowers and he was leaning over the long bench with his back to me and didn't hear me come in, I guess. It looked like he was writing. Anyway he had a pen in his hand and after what I'd just heard it gave me the willies enough without his jumping as though he'd been shot, and dropping his pen when I said hello. And he scared me half out of my wits by snarling at me:

"What are you doing here?"

He didn't even wait for me to answer, but got down on his hands and knees on the dusty floor and began looking for the pen as though it was a diamond or something and he had to find it. When anybody makes me mad I'm just as likely to get perverse as not. I'd seen where the pen had rolled to, back under the bench in a dark corner but I thought, the nasty old thing, I'm not going to pick it up for him, and then all of a sudden I thought about the threatening letter to Mr. Greene and about how Mark and Mr. Richmond didn't seem quite sure it was Mr. Willoughby who had written it and maybe having his pen might help them so I got down fast and pretended to be looking, too. All I had to do, of course, was keep an eye on him and the minute his head was turned I picked it up and stuck it down the front of me, thanking heaven the elastic in my brassiere was good and tight. It wasn't too easy, anyway, because the cap had come off, somewhere, in the shuffle and there I was thinking what a mess I'd be in if the thing stabbed me, all of a sudden, or began to leak.

After a while he had to give up looking for it and tried to pretend it didn't matter, but you could see he was terribly jittery and I was beginning to be pretty much afraid of him anyway. He always was a close-mouthed, quiet sort of man who didn't have much to do with any of us kids, ever, and I couldn't help thinking, my heavens, I wonder what he's like—really—way down inside. But I hadn't come over for any of all that, of course, so I said,

"Mother sent me to pick up your jars and crocks to put the flowers in."

"What flowers?" He was positively shaking.

"For the Festival," I said. "She's in charge of decoration."

He'd been looking at me fairly sharp and I kept thinking, goodness, I wonder if he can see the pen right through my blouse, but I knew it wasn't the time to lose my nerve now and after a little he just gave a sort of hmph!—and said,

"Well, if you want them, I suppose I'll have to help you carry them," and he stooped down and began pulling things from under the bench.

He carried them out and put them in the car for me and I kept wondering what on earth was going on in his head and it hit me like a flash to see what he'd do about it and I said:

"Mr. Richmond's sick."

He stood still, holding a big jar and I thought for a minute he was going to drop it, but he didn't. He just said, "I'm not surprised," and put the crock in the car.

It was the last one, and I stepped on the starter and was just going to shift when I felt his hand on my arm. You can imagine how that made me jump, and then the way he was poking at me, too.

"Young lady, there's going to be trouble at this Festival tonight. If you know what's good for you, you'll stay away from it." He stared at me and the goose flesh started coming out all over my arms. "If you know what's good for you . . ." he said again and turned around and went back around the house toward the tool shed.

If anybody else says anything creepy to me, I thought, I'm going to scream. Right in their faces! And I felt I absolutely had to get down to the boat where Mark must have been expecting me for the last half hour, and I thought how on earth am I going to bear getting on board the *Lark* and then I remembered that anyway *he'd* be with me and I drove up to the porch and Mother said:

"Oh, there you are, dear! Hilda and I'll help you take the jars out and then I want you to run right along over to Herrods' and get somebody to cut delphinium and phlox for you. I only want the Formosum and the Baron Van Dedum. Remember—no Belladonna or Elizabeth Campbell, though if Henrietta's around she'll try to get you to take some. But I will not use light blue and salmon pink with scarlet and deep blue. If I'm going to do all the work this year I'm going to do the planning, too, for once . . ."

Oh my heavens, I thought, will I *ever* get down to the boat? Mark will think I've absolutely eloped and then Mother said something else and I stopped to hear what it was.

"It's certainly nice of that young man to let you use his car like this, and I do hate to put you to so much trouble, dear, but there just isn't a soul I can call on, the way things are, and maybe he'd like to go along."

"Where?" I said. My foot was on the running board.

"Didn't you hear a word, dear? Well, never mind. I can tell you just as well when you get back from Herrods'. I was only saying we *do* need that quilt of Mrs. Carver's and Edith has to have the ship's model for her booth, too, so if you wouldn't mind running in to Mrs. Mack's, poor woman."

"Oh, Mother, I'm sorry. I've got them both here in the car. I just forgot to give them to you, that's all."

"Well, for goodness sake! That's two things off my mind. It does seem to me, Katherine, that you might have been a little more considerate. I'm sure I don't know what on earth's come over everybody this year . . ."

18

Of course I couldn't really blame Mother for being a little impatient with me and I suppose if I'd been in her place I'd been a whole lot crosser than she was. But I couldn't help wondering, too, how she'd like it if things were the other way around and she knew all the horrible things about people that I knew. And how she would feel about the Festival if Mark told her what he'd told me and she'd had Mr. Willoughby glare at her that way and say what he did.

Anyway, the whole business had made me pretty jumpy, I guess, and when I turned into the Herrods' driveway I certainly had the jitters. I never did like the Herrods' house or the grounds, either, from the time I was a little girl. Not in front, anyway. I remember when I was about thirteen I got the idea it was haunted one year because I was reading *Jane Eyre,* and the house was so big and gloomy, with all those Norway pines up close around it, making it dark and damp even on bright days. And then, the way it's built of stone like a year 'round place instead of shingles or logs just for summer the way the others are. Mother used to send me over once in a while to borrow something or I'd just wander that way hoping Les or Arch would be around to play tennis with or swim. I was kind of scared of Les anyway, of course, because he was four

years older than I was. And I'd go up that long avenue of
pines and the screened porch was so shaded I couldn't see
whether anybody was on it or not, and if Mrs. Herrod was
there I'd jump half out of my skin when she boomed at me
the way she always did.

Nobody was on the porch, though, when I scooted up
the drive in the little yellow car and parked in front of
the stone steps. I opened the screen door and walked in
and called Mrs. Herrod but nobody answered and I went
on along the hall and into the big living room with the
French doors. As near as I could make out the house was
absolutely empty. It made me feel funny, wandering like
that through the Herrods' house and none of the Herrods
knowing I was there. Well, I thought, I've got to get those
flowers, and I went on back out to the car and picked up
the two baskets I'd brought with me and the scissors and
the gloves and walked clear around the house along the
brick path to the gardens.

I'd never felt the same way about the gardens I did
about the rest of the house. For one thing they were all
open and sunny and then they were so absolutely beautiful
they made you catch your breath every time you saw them.
I remember Mother told me once they'd been there when
the Herrods—the old people, that is—had first moved
into the place and that old Mrs. Herrod had kept them up
and improved them, too. But young Mrs. Herrod—Henrietta, that is—had let them run down again until Fred
Mack started to work for the Herrods. He'd simply slaved,
bringing them back, and they'd been lovely again for the
past few years.

I couldn't see anybody in the garden, either, and I didn't
want to start cutting flowers without asking Mrs. Herrod,
even though I knew Mother had probably told her I'd be
over. I never had gotten over being afraid of Mrs. Herrod
and she was perfectly nasty, always, about anything she

called impertinence. I couldn't see her any place, though, and I had to get those flowers or Mother'd be having fits and time was going by terribly fast and I wanted to get to the boat, too, so I put my baskets down and started cutting the scarlet phlox. I knew Mother needed all she could get, and, besides, the end of the season was just two days off and the Herrods would be going home so I cut straight down the rows, taking all there were.

The phlox just about filled both baskets I'd brought and I still had to get the dark delphinium—there was simply tons of it. I certainly didn't want to go home after more baskets and I knew the Herrods must have a lot of things like that in the tool house, the way everybody did, so I went back there and walked in. I was feeling worse and worse about mussing around with other people's things when they weren't there—specially the Herrods—but I figured I wasn't hurting anything, really. The baskets were all standing under the wide shelf where the small garden tools were kept—little ones up in front and some big ones, the kind I needed, behind them, way at the back. I had to move a whole batch of little ones and get practically under the shelf, on my hands and knees to find what I was after. I reached in and took hold of a nice, fat one that was made of split basswood and pulled it out and then the one back of that and underneath it, in the dark there, I saw something small and white and my heart jumped right up in my throat because I knew what it was. It was Alicia's purse that Helen Willoughby had picked up on the beach that night only it was all soiled with lying in the dirt that way.

I thought, my goodness, I'm making a regular collection for Mark today and picked it up, so you can imagine how I jumped when Mrs. Herrod's voice boomed out.

"Katherine Edwards! What are you up to now?"

I absolutely screamed. I couldn't help it.

"Oh!" I said, "I'm sorry, Mrs. Herrod. You scared me."

"I should hope so! Just what do you think you're doing?"

She positively glared at me, but I was getting so sick and tired of being yelled at when I was just doing what I was supposed to that I got mad and when I get mad enough I forget to be afraid any longer.

"I'm getting flowers," I said, "for the Festival. For Mother! Goodness knows nobody else is helping her!"

Mrs. Herrod actually snorted. "Flowers!" she said. "Under that bench!"

"No. I was trying to find some baskets to put them in."

" . . . rummaging around! On other people's property!" I was still holding Alicia's purse, of course, and she pointed her finger at it like some horrible, avenging fate. "And is *that* what you call a basket?" Mr. Herrod had come up when he heard all the row, I suppose, and he was standing behind her looking henpecked and half scared, too, the way he usually did, but I didn't care any longer.

"No! It isn't what I'd call a basket, but that's where I found it—under there in all that dirt. You know perfectly well that it's Alicia Richmond's purse that Helen Willoughby picked up on the beach the night Alicia died and that it had her keys in it—the keys to the cabin of the *Lark*. Somebody was on board the *Lark* last night, after Mr. Richmond left it, and I guess . . . I guess I know who it was . . ."

Mrs. Herrod's face just sort of dropped open—that's the only thing you could call it—and then it all tightened up and I saw Leslie, looking terribly white, standing behind her in the doorway.

"This is the most impertinent thing I've ever heard! Are you accusing me—*me* of groveling in the dirt with any of that girl's belongings?" She drew herself up very tall. "I will *not* be held responsible . . ." And then she saw Les.

I thought, My goodness, he's a man but he's going to faint. He didn't, though. He just stood looking at her and she stared back at him and then dropped her eyes and I couldn't stand any more of it.

"I don't want any of your flowers!" I said. "I don't want anything of yours! I don't want anything more to do with you or the Willoughbys. Ever. And I won't go to your nasty Festival tonight. You're horrible . . . horrible!"

I turned and ran with my head down out of the shed, not seeing anything, and I bumped slam bang into Arch and he caught my arm and held me.

"What's the row, Kitty?" He seemed so good and decent, somehow, after all these others, and I was just about ready to break, too. Anyway, I started crying like a sap and he went along with me around the house and. when I opened the door of the Fiat I saw that he had the two baskets of phlox and my gloves and the scissors he must have picked up in the garden where I'd left them.

"Get hold of yourself, Kitty," he said. "You can't give in now, you know. Somebody's got to keep you from making a silly little fool of yourself the way Crosby kept me from making a fool of myself a few days ago. Buck up! You've got to go through with the Festival. Every bit of it! We all do."

I was mopping my eyes and feeling pretty much ashamed. I knew he was right and I thought he was being pretty swell.

"O. K., Arch," I said. "I won't do it again. It's only . . ."

"I know. Now listen. There's no sense letting the whole countryside know my mother's on a rampage. What flowers do you still need? Delphinium? All right, I'll see you get 'em. The Festival starts at eight and we've got to make a showing if the world busts wide open. Understand?"

"Thanks, Arch. Only the Formosum . . ."

"All right. Now listen here. You fix your face up and take the phlox home to your mother and then go on down to the *Lark*. Crosby's fit to be tied. Afraid something's happened to you. That's why I came up—to see if I could find you for him. Tell your mother I'll have her delphinium for her not later than six o'clock. She can count on me. And tell Crosby everything's set—we'll be along. He can count on me, too."

"Who's 'we'?" I said. "Who'll be along?" But all I could do, really, was remember the look Arch had given me that day on the beach when I'd thought he meant to let me know he understood and I wasn't sure. And I was glad clear down inside me because I knew, now, that Arch was on our side, too.

"Who'll be along?" I said again, but Arch just shook his head and smiled a strange, unhappy sort of a smile, and started walking away from me back toward the gardens where I'd left his mother and father and Les a little while before.

"Just tell Crosby what I said. He'll understand."

19

I didn't really mean what I'd said to Mrs. Herrod—about knowing who had been on board the *Lark* the night before. The truth was I didn't know any more than I ever had. It was just that I was mad and wanted to hit out at somebody. In fact I was more mixed up and confused, even, than I'd been all along. It seemed to me nothing made sense.

The last person I'd seen with Alicia's purse was Helen Willoughby, and it certainly was pretty obvious that it had been Mr. Willoughby who had written that letter about the Greene place. The trouble was, I didn't see how the letter and the purse connected. If Helen had carried it home and her father had taken the keys out of it, I wouldn't have found it in the Herrods' tool shed, would I? And then it struck me like a light that of course it's just the sort of thing Mr. Willoughby would have done with it to throw people off the track. But what on earth was he doing on board the *Lark*, anyway?

You can see the state I must have been in by the time I got down to the boat. I'd had to go home first and I knew Arch was right, saying there wasn't any sense letting the whole country know his mother was on a rampage—if that's what he wanted to call it. I certainly had to keep *my* mother from knowing or she'd be right over at Herrods' to see what was the matter. And Mrs. Herrod would tell her how impertinent I'd been and I'd never in the world make Mother see how I felt about it all because she'd say that was just Henrietta and I ought to know better. But I knew—I absolutely knew right down inside me—that it wasn't just Henrietta, or if it was she was a whole lot worse than anybody'd ever thought she was. Why, she's horrible, I thought. She's simply poisonous.

I fixed my face with powder and some fresh make-up and I was awfully thankful Mother was so busy she didn't have time to notice I'd been crying, since it wasn't too obvious by then. I drove up to the house and jumped out fast so she'd think I was just in a hurry and told her Arch would bring the delphinium over—I hadn't had room in the baskets—and that I was going on down to the Rich- monds' boat to see Mark for a minute.

"Well, do hurry dear, won't you? I'll be out of my mind by eight o'clock the way things are. It just seems to me we can't get the Festival going at all without Fred around to help. Last year he did everything—absolutely everything. He always has. And Henrietta! She's usually running the whole thing, and now, this year . . . I can't think what's come over her. Her bridge was way off last night—if you can call it bridge with all that jumping up and running around. Arch had to sit in twice. And as for Leslie . . ."

I asked her what jumping up and running around and usually she'd have spent fifteen minutes, if I'd listened, telling me all about it but she just threw up her hands and said, "Kitty, dear—can't you see I can't talk now? Run along, dear—and hurry. Anyway, it's of no consequence . . ." and she was off into the house, her heels clicking brisk and busy across the floor.

Mark was standing waiting for me when I drove along the dock to the *Lark*. He must have changed when he took Mr. Richmond home, I thought, because he was in ducks

and it was the first time I'd seen him like that and he was
so darned good-looking it slayed me. His tan was a simply
luscious mahogany color and you know how that looks
with white clothes. When he held out both hands to me
and took hold of mine he was stuttering like a magpie.

"F-f-for God's sake, K-k-kathie—where the hell have
you b-b-b-b . . ."

"Been!" I said. "Where haven't I? Everybody's left Mother completely flat and the Festival's supposed to start at
eight and I've been running all over for her. I've had a simply terrible set-to with Mrs. Herrod and finding Alicia's
purse there and all, and then Mr. Willoughby sailing into
me that way and—oh, Mark! I'm absolutely sure he wrote
that letter and if you'd seen us both scrambling around on
the floor there after his pen . . ." I began to giggle. "You
see, when he dropped it, I saw where it fell, and all of a
sudden I thought how smart it would be if I picked it up
and brought it to you. It might help you make really sure
he'd written that letter. So I did . . ."

I'd been rattling on just the way Mother does when she
gets excited and I was out of breath. It's only that I was so
tickled to see him and I had so much to tell him I didn't
know where to begin.

"So I see," he said and I noticed he wasn't looking at
me but at the front of me and that the corners of his
mouth were twinkling the way they do when he's going to
smile one of those big ones.

I looked down and there was that darned pen sticking
right up out of my blouse just about ready to fall and
I blushed awfully and then I remembered how Mr. Willoughby had stared at me and I thought, good heavens! I
wonder how long it's been that way.

"Come on," Mark said, "Pull yourself together. You're
talking gibberish. We'll go on board and you can sit down

and tell me just what happened. But first maybe you'd better give me those two treasures you've cadged for me. Before you lose 'em."

I handed him the pen and the purse, too, and he swung himself on board and helped me up and pulled out two deck chairs and we sat down, facing shore.

"Now, out with it," he said. "And try beginning at the beginning. That sometimes helps."

So I told him about the Herrods and Mr. Willoughby and what Bill Hennebery had said.

"Kathie! You're a wonder. We make a swell team. Because while I've been digging up facts you've been right in there getting the lay of the land."

I suppose my face must have showed that that wasn't what I thought I'd been doing at all, because he smiled at me in that quick, warm way of his.

"You see, Kathie, what you've brought me is a purse from a hiding place and a pen that Mr. Willoughby had in his hand. The purse may have been any place—in the possession of half a dozen people—since now and the time you saw it last, and the pen may not be Mr. Willoughby's at all. A pen without a cap . . ."

It all made me feel perfectly useless, as though I'd bungled things.

"Mark," I said, "please . . . let me go back there and look again. You see, I was in such a hurry . . . maybe I could find the cap."

"Swell!" Mark said. "Unless, of course he has picked it up himself in the meantime. I won't pretend it may not be important. But don't worry about it too much. What you *have* brought me is a whole lot more important, at this stage of the game. You've brought me news that the enemy is weakening. They've got the jitters. It's what I've been waiting for. It wasn't until the supporting opposition began to crack that I could go in there and break them down.

"We're closing in, Kathie. The big fight is just ahead. Now let's have a look at what's in this purse."

He turned it upside down over my lap. There wasn't much in it. Just a crumpled handkerchief and a bobbie pin or two and a cigarette case and a lip stick and a compact and that was all.

"Keys gone, of course," he said. "Is there a monogram on any of the junk?"

"Yes, on all of it. Block letters. A. R. See—even the lip stick. The cigarette case is all curlycues, though, one of those nasty ones I never can make out. Oh yes, it's *A. R.*, too, but there's another letter . . . it looks like an *H*. It couldn't be *H* though, could it?"

The corners of Mark's mouth were twinkling. "Oh yes," he said, "it could. Anything can happen in this strangest of worlds. You told me yourself, didn't you, that Alicia was married once?"

"Of course!" I felt absolutely stupid. *"Hunter.* Alicia Richmond Hunter."

"A. R. H." Mark said. "Yes, so it is." He wasn't exactly smiling, but the way he looked it struck me he was having some fun about something I wasn't in on.

"I don't know what you and Arch are up to," I said. "All I know is he asked me to tell you 'Everything's set—we'll be along.' Just like that! And that you could count on him. He wouldn't tell me who'd be along or another thing about it. He said you'd know."

I knew I was acting silly, sulking at being left in the dark like that, and I suppose he figured I'd be glad to snap out of it if he'd just give me a helping hand. Anyway, he looked serious enough when he said, "Thanks, Kathie. Yes, I know. And I know you'll forgive us when it's over for not letting you in. It seemed the best way to play it, that's all."

He glanced up over the rail and out at the water and the shore and then looked down again at the pen that seemed awfully small and unimportant, somehow, after all the fuss I'd made about it, lying in the palm of his big hand.

"Willoughby's in chemicals," he said. "Right?"

"Yes, Henry Willoughby, Incorporated, you know."

He nodded. "I suppose Willoughby usually has a lot of drugs around—insecticides, things like that?"

"Why yes. They've always sold stuff to everybody up here wholesale. It used to be Willoughby and Starck in his father's time and before that just Starck and Sons."

"Starck and Sons. Yes, I know, I traced back on all that ancient history in town before I came up. Starck and Sons . . ."

"G-g-good Lord, K-k-kathie! I think I've got the missing piece. And none too soon. If it weren't for a kind providence I'd have been dead long ago, the length of time it takes my mind, sometimes, to put two and two together and make four. You know that bottle Fred started to make the ship's model in . . ."

He stopped, all of a sudden, and just stood there and for the first time since I'd known him he looked as though he couldn't make up his mind which way to go. Then he pulled himself, together and grew terribly solemn.

"Kathie! Something's going to happen in about a minute that may scare the daylights out of you. Try not to be afraid. It's all right. Honest it is."

And that's all the warning I had before he left me and went forward into the cabin and I heard Alicia Richmond, her voice clear and sad the way it had been the night she died, singing, "You'll take the high road."

I couldn't make a sound. It was just like in a nightmare when a scream gets stuck back in your throat that's closed up tight with horror. And I couldn't move. All I could do was sit there, hanging on tight to the wooden arms of the deck chair and stare out over the rail to where I could see Arch and Les coming together along the beach. I saw Les stand stock-still for a minute and then start down the dock toward the *Lark* with something fast and desperate in the way he walked, like a man who knows there's a precipice just ahead and that when he gets there he'll have to jump.

20

It didn't take me long, actually, to realize where Alicia's voice must be coming from or Les, either, I suppose, but it seemed like ages because it was pretty awful to be listening to a girl who was dead singing like that on the boat that had carried her body.

"Les!" I said, "Leslie!" when he swung himself on board. But he went by me as though he didn't even know I was there and Arch had reached the boat by that time, too, and I felt the pressure of his hand on my arm, reassuringly for a second, before he followed me down the companionway into the cabin.

It was dim in there after the brightness of the open deck with only the four brass-bound portholes staring out at the sky, and for a minute I couldn't see a thing. But I heard the needle scraping on the record and Alicia's throaty, sad contralto singing, "Oh, me and my true love will never meet again," and then I saw Mark beside a radio-phonograph that was built into the wall, and Les standing there absolutely glaring at him.

"What the hell did you do that for, Crosby? Where did you get that record?"

Mark kept on looking at him, and didn't say a word.

"Crosby! For God's sake . . ."

163

I suppose it was about then that he began to realize what he'd let himself in for and you could see him trying to pull himself together. He took out a cigarette and tapped it, taking his time, and struck a match, but his hand was shaking so that he could hardly light it.

"Gave you a jolt, did it?" Mark said. "Hearing her voice again?"

"What's wrong with that? Give anybody a jolt. Look at Kitty . . ."

Of course I wasn't in such good shape yet myself, but just the same I knew that there was something different about the way I was feeling and the way Les was.

"Never mind Kitty. And never mind where I got the record. It's on the market as you very well know. And as for why I played it as you were passing—it seems to me that's obvious, too."

"Sure! To stir up trouble. That's what you're all about. Why don't you mind your own business?"

"And why don't you come clean and tell the truth?"

But Les had got hold of himself and you could see he'd made up his mind to fight it through.

"The truth?" he said, and he managed to make his voice pretty ironic. "That's good, coming from you. How about a little truth on your side. What are you doing up here? What are you after?"

The record had come to an end and Mark had turned his back and was lifting the needle off. As he snapped the stop on the machine he swung around and his face and voice were pretty grim.

"Don't try to cross-examine me!" he said. "That's my game. Where were you, Leslie Herrod, on the night of October 13th . . ."

Les tried to laugh. "Oh, come now, Crosby! Suppose I asked you where you were on some arbitrary date eight years ago."

Mark smiled. "Eight years ago! I didn't say a word about eight years ago. Trapped yourself, didn't you? The old conscience got right in there and tripped you up, because it was eight years ago, wasn't it?"

Leslie's eyes shifted. There hadn't been much color in his face from the beginning but all the rest of it seemed to have drained away.

"Don't bother answering, Les, because I know. You were in a night club with Gerry Hunter."

"All right," Les said. "What if I was?"

"You were in a night club with Gerry Hunter and you heard Alicia sing for the first time. You and Gerry had come down from school together for the express purpose of raising general hell."

"O. K. Then what? General hell is something a lot of men in college raise on week ends once in a while, but that doesn't mean they have to answer questions about it afterwards, on the stand."

"Not unless they get themselves in a jam, Leslie. And let their friends in for it, too. Not unless they see a girl like Alicia Richmond and hear her sing and decide that, since she's an entertainer, she's anybody's game."

When Leslie laughed that time I thought, he's getting that laugh in pretty good control.

"Oh, now I see what you're driving at, Crosby. I'm sorry, you've got your stories mixed. It was Gerry who got in the jam. Gerry went after her. I just tagged along."

"You just tagged along, did you, while Gerry found out who she was and where she lived? All about her family and the schools she'd gone to and the fact that her father had given in to letting her sing in public because her mother had died without a chance to use her voice?

"You just tagged along! Well, maybe you did—I wouldn't know how much you let Gerry cover for you from the start. But you weren't tagging along after you found out she wasn't anybody's game. After you'd started going after her in earnest—seeing her every night you could get away from school, sending her presents . . ."

"There's no law against that!"

"No, there's no law against that. But there is a law against a minor's marrying without his parents' consent. And a law that says those parents can have a marriage like that annulled if the kids pull a fast one and put it over. And there was a law in your school—a hard and fast one—against the marriage of undergraduates. If you did it and you were found out you were expelled. And you knew it."

I suppose Les must have been concentrating everything he had on keeping his feet because I'm sure he didn't see the look that Mark gave Arch or notice when Arch slipped out on deck. He took a long drag at his cigarette and followed the glowing end with his eyes, smiling a little as though the whole thing amused him some but bored him more.

"Oh, come now, Crosby, you sound like my mother when she gets on a tear. What's all this got to do with me? I don't know what you're digging it up for, but whatever is on your mind, you're barking up the wrong tree. Maybe I was pretty excited about Alicia—but so was Gerry. And Gerry won—that's all. It's Gerry who got in the jam. Not me. Why don't you ask him. about it?"

He must have heard them crossing the deck because he turned around and then he saw Gerry standing there with Arch in the cabin doorway.

"Hello, Les," Gerry said.

It gave Les time to get hold of himself and he sounded pretty normal when he said:

"Hi, Gerry! When did you get up? I thought you told me in town . . ."

Gerry said, "Yes, I know. Look here, Les . . . It had to come out some time. The minute Richmond came into the picture up here, it was all over. You know that. So when Crosby wired me you were ready to break . . ."

Les threw the end of his cigarette down on the cabin floor and stamped it out, and the blood rushed up red in his face and he started toward Mark and I saw his fist shoot out and Mark grab his wrist and throw him, and I gave a funny, little low moan and covered my eyes and I heard a chair go over and a body banging against a wall and then it was all quiet for a minute except for the sound of somebody breathing hard and Mark's voice saying:

"Can you hang onto him a minute while he calms down?" and then, "Here, Kathie—here's a drink." And I opened my eyes and Mark was bending over me and there was brandy, warm and stinging on my lips and in my throat.

Les said, "Give me a drink. And lay off. I'm all right now."

He was sitting on the long bench on the starboard side, and Gerry and Arch were holding him and Gerry looked up at Mark and said, "O. K.?" and Mark nodded and filled another glass.

"Les," he said, and held it out and all I could see was pity and understanding in his eyes. Les must have seen it, too, because he said, "Thanks, Crosby," and took the brandy in one swallow and held out the glass. "Better give me another," he said.

Mark poured one all around and then he sat down on the bench opposite Les and said quietly:

"You can see for yourself, Les, that Richmond must have told me the whole story before I ever came up."

"Richmond!" Gerry said. "If Richmond hadn't acted like such a damned, unreasonable fool, there wouldn't have been any trouble."

"Hold on a minute, Hunter. Wait till all the evidence is in. You married her, didn't you, Les?"

Les said, "Yes."

"And then she told her father."

"And her father blew up with all on board!" Gerry cut in again. "You'd think Les was poison or something. If he hadn't raised all that row . . ."

"As far as Richmond was concerned, Les *was* poison."

"Why?" Les said. "That's what I want to know. Why? Even my mother wouldn't . . . oh Lord!" He groaned.

"Sure, Les, I know." Mark sounded as though he was talking to a little boy who'd hurt himself. "I know, your mother raised a row, too, didn't she? Only you never let Gerry know. You let him think the whole thing was Richmond's fault all along. You've never let him know that you might have tried to fight it out with Richmond if you'd had your mother back of you. And that it wasn't until she raised hell, too, and told you . . ."

"She told me that it was life and death—that nobody must ever know we'd married. She told me I had to find some way out of it—keep even the annulment from being known. She—she's pretty terrifying when she gets going strong . . . you don't know, Crosby . . ."

"O. K. And there was the school outfit right on your neck and Gerry'd been a witness, so you dug up the old mixed identity gag."

"Hell!" Gerry said. "What did I have to lose? I didn't have any folks and my guardian was a good guy. He took the whole thing in his stride, and it pulled Les out of a hole."

"It pulled Les out of a hole and put you in one," Mark said, "when you came up here and met Tess and had to deal with the man-about-town reputation you'd earned because Mrs. Herrod spread the story fast that Gerry Hunter had been kicked out of school for marrying a night club girl."

"It was all right with Tess," Gerry said, "until the Richmonds came along and I found myself in a spot. I had to play up to Alicia—do my piece—or let Les down. And I couldn't tell Tess a damned thing except that it was all Richmond's fault. Because I thought it was."

Les hadn't said a word for five minutes. When he looked up at Mark now you could see he was pretty beaten.

"For God's sake, Crosby, tell me something. What was poison about me to Richmond?"

"The same thing," Mark said, "that was poison about Alicia to your mother. Gossip! Scandal! Talk! Talk that got going when Alicia's mother died. Talk that drove Richmond out of here twenty-five years ago and sent him back to fight.

"Les, your mother and Mr. Richmond have had one thing in common all these years. They've both more than half believed the gossip that Richmond wasn't Alicia's father. And that your father was!"

I drew in my breath sharp and looked at Leslie and I sat there simply fascinated watching the change that came over his face. It was as though he was seeing something he didn't want to see and he couldn't help seeing it because it was there, right in front of him, staring back. And Mark's voice cut in, hard and sure,

"Who was on this boat last night?"

But Les only shook his head.

"I saw the light," Mark hammered at him, "And I saw you slip down off the dock onto the rocks and swim for the *Felicity* after the light went out.

"And I waited for you to come back . . ."

Leslie was shaking as though he had a chill.

"For God's sake, Crosby. Let up. What are you pounding at me for? You know who it was, don't you? You know I followed her down from the house when she left. You know it was my mother."

21

It was a perfectly awful time for my name to come streaming in through the cabin windows in my own mother's
high, clear voice.

"Katherine!" she called. "Kath-er-ine!" and I knew that
any minute she'd be saying, "Oh, there you are, dear. My
goodness! I've been looking simply everywhere for you."
And then probably, in another second, something about
Henrietta . . .

I felt as if I couldn't stand it to talk to her just as
though nothing had happened, and get busy about the
Festival again—remembering every time I saw Henrietta
Herrod or even thought about her, what was hidden under
her importance and respectability. And how ghastly it was
going to be when it all came out. Because I don't care how
much you hate somebody or even if you've been afraid of
them ever since you were a kid, it's something else again
to think of them as being tried for murder.

There wasn't a sound in the cabin of the *Lark* except
the voices of the children coming from shore and the staccato beat of an outboard somewhere on the bay and the
water slapping against the boat's sides and the quick tap-
tap of my mother's heels along the planking of the dock.

Mark said, "Snap out of it! Every one of you! Pull
yourselves together," and then, "Take it easy, Les. Take it

easy . . ." and he was up the companionway in three steps and out on deck talking to my mother as though everything was just fine.

He was saying, "Sorry, Mrs. Edwards, we got talking," when the rest of us followed him up and I looked at Mother standing there and I thought how darned good and sweet she was, and I knew that if Mark could help it he wouldn't hurt her for the world.

He smiled his nice big smile at her and swung himself over the rail and she went absolutely feminine:

"I don't *mean* to be cross," she said. "It's just that there's so much still to do, Mr. Crosby, even though Tess has shown up again and Helen and Ruth. Though where on earth Vinny's gone . . . and now Edith Willoughby's upset because Henry has locked himself in his room and just keeps saying he's not going to stir out of it for anybody. So if some of you men could help me just a little . . ."

"How about it, Gerry?" Mark said. "Figure Tess wouldn't mind your giving her a hand . . . along about now?"

". . . and Henrietta hasn't sent me that delphinium yet," Mother said. "She promised she'd have it over . . ."

Mark caught Leslie's eye and kept looking at him hard. "Les can round that up for you, can't you, Les?"

Les looked as though he couldn't even round himself up, let alone face his mother and get delphinium out of her. But my mother was all smoothed down and happy as a bird, walking those quick little steps of hers on ahead of us up the dock. Les just stood there.

"You won't do your mother any good going to pieces like that," Mark said.

"Oh, my God . . . my mother . . ."

Mark closed his fingers tight on Leslie's arm. "Keep your chin up," he said, and dropped back to where I was waiting beside his car.

"Handy little item—that bit of information your mother tossed out about Willoughby."

I thought, Oh dear, I suppose it was silly of me to hope things would quiet down for a little. Long enough, anyway, for me to get my breath.

"What's handy about it? It seems to me it just helps gum things up."

"All depends on how you look at it. If you mean it'll make the Festival harder to get under way, you're probably right, but if it should happen to strike you as it does me you'll see it gives us each a swell opportunity for action."

"Action?" I said, and then it hit me, too. "You mean I can go mussing around in the Willoughby's tool shed looking for that pen cap without running into him?"

"Right! And in case you're still jumpy about his catching up with you, I can ease your mind by telling you that while you're hunting on the outskirts I'll be right in there bearding him in his den."

"You're going to talk to Mr. Willoughby?"

"No—I'm going to make him talk. He's hiding out—and shaking in his boots. Which is a fact I'm going to take every advantage of."

"What about Mrs. Herrod, Mark? What are you going to do . . . ?"

"The first thing I'm going to do," he said, "is park this car. There are times when you can move faster on foot than you can on wheels. And this is one of them. Besides, I want to take a look-in and see how Richmond's getting along and if the good doctor is any place around.

"Don't worry about Mrs. Herrod, Kathie. We'll deal with her when it fits. Things are shaping fine."

Shaping fine, I thought, for trouble! I could absolutely feel it in the air. The sun shone with a brassy light and the leaves of the trees were limp and sorry-looking and the

golden-rod and wild asters were gray with dust. Of course
there hadn't been any rain for nearly two weeks, which
was one reason why Mother and everybody was expecting
a storm, but it wasn't only that. It was just that everything
that had happened was making me see past the surface of
the way I'd always thought things were and realize that
it wasn't Alicia who had brought trouble to Sidley's Cove
but Sidley's Cove that had something mean and hateful
underneath like an ugly growth. And it made me feel all
sick inside to know it was still there, festering, and that it
had to be brought out into the light and destroyed before
things would ever be right again.

All the horrible, gloomy pines scowled down at us from
in front of the Herrods' as we passed and I thought how
silly and pretentious the gingerbready scrollwork looked
along the gable ends at the Willoughbys', and it seemed to
me that only our house and the Conovers' and the new log
ones that people like the Arnolds were beginning to put up
were plain and simple.

Mark had stopped under the porte-cochere at the side
of the Greene place, and it struck me that it wouldn't be
so bad if the people who lived in it had a time of being
happy for a change and ripped some of the verandas off
and opened the windows to the sun.

Dr. Carver was just coming down the steps in that quick,
hurrying way of his. He looked worried and as though he
wasn't a bit sure, for his part, that things were shaping
fine at all. He stopped when he saw us and said, "Hello,
Katherine," and shook his head. "I don't know, Crosby. I
don't know . . ."

Mark frowned. "What's the matter? Richmond worse?"

"No-o-o—not worse. Think maybe we'll pull him
through. Mrs. Conover's on the job. Fine nurse! Fine
woman! But I don't like it. I'm not sure all this undercover
business is getting us anywhere."

"O. K." Mark said. "Want to pull out?"

"We-ell . . ." Dr. Carver put his bag down on the gravel drive and felt around in his pocket for his pipe. "You see, Crosby, it was different before when we didn't have anything but a lot of guesswork to go on. I had to agree with you that chronology of respiration and pulse cessation may indicate a lot, but just because a girl stops breathing before her heart gives out isn't anything you can get a hanging on. In Richmond's case, though, it's different. I could turn in 'with homicidal intent' all right after what I got today."

"On the part of whom? . . . person or persons unknown?"

"Oh, come now, Crosby . . ."

"O. K. But it's got to be proved. And that's what I'm out to do—fast. Stand by me a little longer, doctor—if you can."

"I don't know . . . Brownlow saw what happened in my office. He's got a brain."

He drew at his pipe and stood holding the bowl cupped in the palm of his hand. When he looked up at Mark his eyes were friendly but they were shrewd too.

"Coroner's got his own office to think of, you know, Crosby. There's Brownlow and Stewart . . . and the township . . . Tell you what—I'll hold off this afternoon. But tomorrow morning I'll have to turn in a report."

"Swell!" Mark said. "That's all I ask. Meantime, I wonder if you'd like to do another piece of laboratory work?"

He had the pen in his hand.

"What have you got there?" Dr. Carver said, eyeing it suspiciously as though he thought Mark was up to something like trying to distract him with a child's toy.

"Surely, doctor, you haven't forgotten the Henry Hoch case."

It was the first time in my life, as far as I could remember, that I'd ever heard Dr. Carver whistle. It was a long, thin whistle of what I suppose is called astonishment.

"You don't say . . . !" His eyes crinkled at the corners and he looked at Mark with what I could only think of as amused admiration. "Smart, aren't you?"

"Don't give me the credit—Kathie picked it up."

"Where? Where'd she find it?"

"In Willoughby's tool shed—Willoughby dropped it from his hand."

Dr. Carver frowned. "I don't see . . . Has the sack been removed?"

"No. Sack's there all right, filled with a clear, colorless fluid, practically odorless . . ."

"Whe-ew! The pure alkaloid—eh?"

"That's what I'd like you to check on. And, doctor, do you think you can get it to me a little after eight?"

"Certainly, Crosby. Where'll you be?"

"Oh, milling around the Festival. I suppose I can count on Brownlow and Stewart to show up there, too."

"Undoubtedly," Dr. Carver said. "Complete with families."

"Fine! If things go the way I think they will, I'm going to make my big play in the presence of the law."

22

If I'd thought for one second there was going to be a single breathing space for the rest of that afternoon, I was certainly wrong. The minute Dr. Carver got into his car and headed out of the Richmonds' driveway, Mark said:

"Come on, Kathie, we've got to work fast. You take the path and I'll take the road and we'll close in on Willoughby before he knows there's an enemy in the field."

It had been all very well for me to say I'd go back there to the Willoughbys' tool shed and look for the cap of that pen when doing it was still an hour or more away, but now that I was right up against it, I was scared stiff. The way I felt about Mark, though, I wouldn't have let him see it for the world if I could help it, but I suppose he knew.

He said, "Don't let it get you, Kathie. Take your time— make as sure as you can that nobody sees you. They've seen too much already. And if you do happen to bump into any of the folks, make it 'hello' and 'good-by' and get away. I'll meet you back here at the car."

There was a quick little pressure of his hand in mine and he said, "Good luck, my dear," and left me.

So I took the path that runs along back of the cottages —the one Bill Hennebery uses when he delivers groceries and milk. I didn't see a soul when I passed Conovers' and our house but I heard Gerry's voice calling out something to Tess, and Mother giving orders and having the time of her life. And I kept saying over and over again, "It's all right, everything's going to be all right," while I was going through the little grove in back of the Willoughbys' and around the tool shed on the far side away from the house.

I kept thinking, oh dear, if anybody sees me what will I say, because I must have looked pretty silly down there on my hands and knees on the floor where the pen had dropped and trying to keep an eye on the door at the same time.

And then the dirt—and the spiders! If there's one thing that gives me the creeps, it's spiders and there were simply millions of them and their old dusty webs under the long bench there in the dark. I moved every jar and basket and bottle and flower pot in the place, making a perfectly awful racket, it seemed to me, but I couldn't find the cap. I knew right where the pen had fallen, too, but it certainly wasn't there.

"Oh, dear!" I said, and stood up and began trying to brush the dirt off my dress and my hands and knees. I was a perfect mess and I thought, my heavens, I've got to get home and change before anybody sees me. They'll think I've been playing hide and seek in an abandoned tunnel. So you can see how perfectly natural it was for me to give a little squeal when I heard somebody say:

"Why, Kitty, what's the matter, child?"

And then I laughed because it was only Mr. Herrod standing in a gap in the lilac hedge between the Willoughbys' place and theirs. He looked as though somebody had just slapped his face and, somehow, I felt terribly sorry for him and thought how he probably hadn't had much fun out of life.

"I was looking for something I . . . lost."

"What is it? Perhaps I could help you."

"Oh, it's nothing. Really, Mr. Herrod . . . it's just . . ."
And then the whole thing struck me funny and I said, "You
must think I spend most of my time rummaging around in
other people's tool sheds."

He smiled and patted my arm.

"Didn't you let Henrietta put you out, Kitty. She's all
bark and no bite. You take my word for it. We're going to
watch the fireworks from the *Felicity,* whatever she says."

He sort of winked at me and I knew he thought he was
being reassuring, but I just wished he'd stop rambling on
and let me go. And then I remembered what Mark had said
about if I ran into anybody to make it "hello" and "good-
by" and be on my way.

I said that would be lovely, or something silly like that
because of course I didn't think it would be lovely at all,
but then I told him I was in a hurry, right now, please, and
if I didn't show up pretty soon Mother would be having fits.

"Mind—don't you let Henrietta put you out," he said
and I said, "No, I won't," and finally got away.

I hadn't seen a thing of Mark, of course, from the time
he left me and I ran all the way up the path to the Greene
place, wondering just how important that pen cap was and
feeling perfectly terrible about not having been able to
find it. I could see him through the trees, before I reached
there, walking back and forth with that long, restless
stride of his, beside the Fiat, under the porte-cochere. He
must have heard the twigs snapping as I came through the
underbrush because he looked up.

"K-k-kathie!" he said. "Are y-y-you all right?"

"Of course! Except the mess I'm in." I glanced down
at my dress that was simply filthy with dust and cobwebs
and laughed and held out my dirty hands for him to see. "I
didn't find the pen cap, though. I'm sorry, Mark—really, I
am—I looked *hard.*"

"Never mind the pen cap. I've got it! All I want to be sure of is that you're safe."

"*You've* got it? Oh Mark . . . how?" And then I knew. "Mr. Willoughby picked it up, didn't he? But how on earth did you make him give it to you?"

"I didn't have to make him. He handed it over without a murmur."

"But why?"

"It was a bargain," Mark said. "I promised him safe-conduct in return. So he gave that to me and a piece of highly valuable information I was after, and we parted in a state of truce.

"What I want to know, though, is how you came out. Didn't bump into anybody, did you?"

"Only Mr. Herrod."

"Good Lord!"

"Oh, it was all right, Mark. He just laughed at me and told me not to let Henrietta put me out. We were going to watch the fireworks from the water tonight, no matter what she said—stuff like that . . ."

Mark had my arm and his fingers tightened on it for a second and he said:

"Look, Kathie, I said things were going to happen fast. Well, they're happening almost too damned fast for me. I've got something to tell you—something hellish important. But first I've got to tie up another knot or two. You're safe—so far. And just to be sure you stay safe you're going along with me."

He helped me into the little car and got under the wheel and spun it around and headed down the bay shore road toward town.

"But, Mark," I said, while the wind swirled my hair around my head, "I can't go any place like this! Let me out! I've got to go home and change."

"You'll have time enough to change," he said, "after we've seen Bertha Mack."

23

The Macks' house was an old gray shingle bow roof that
looked as though it had been standing on the waterfront
near the docks where the fishing boats come in since the
first net was lifted off the banks. It had white window trim
and thick, white-painted doors and two huge chimneys
rising above the roof at either end.

I had only been inside it once when I was little and my
Dad had taken me there one day when he wanted to see
Fred. I remembered that I was scared that time, too, because Mrs. Mack was one of those women "that keeps herself to herself," as the Village says, and even when you did
see her on the street or in the store she was never smiling.

I don't suppose you ever do throw off a lot of the way
you feel about people when you're small because I know I
was pretty shaky when Mark rapped the knocker against
the wood of the door and I heard footsteps coming along
the hall.

The door opened, creaking a little on its hinges, and
my heart came right up in my throat when I saw Mrs.
Mack's gaunt, old face peering at us through the narrow
crack.

"Well?" she said.

"Sorry to bother you, Mrs. Mack. I thought perhaps
you'd want to know. Charlie Richmond's sick."

Her face didn't change at all but she opened the door a little wider.

"I suppose you might as well come in."

"Thank you," Mark said, and I didn't see how on earth he kept it from sounding ironic.

She looked at me as though she was seeing me for the first time. "Hmph! It's Katherine Edwards . . ." and she led the way into the parlor that was filled with rich, stuffy old Victorian furniture that seemed terribly out of place in that kind of a house. I wondered where on earth she'd ever managed to find it and why, while we sat down stiffly on the horsehair chairs,

"What's the matter with Charlie?"

"The same thing that was the matter with Fred—somebody tried to murder him. Only this time they didn't quite succeed."

You couldn't tell what she was thinking from the expression of her face but she'd started twisting the wide, gold band of her wedding ring around and around her finger.

"You brought Charlie up, didn't you, Mrs. Mack?"

"Yes, after his mother died. Until he got out of hand."

"His mother was your sister? What do you mean 'got out of hand'?"

"I told him not to mix in with that crowd. I told him no good would come of it. But he wouldn't pay any heed!"

"Why should he? You never gave him a reason. You didn't tell him the truth!"

For a minute she met his eyes, but he stared back at her.

"It's no good, Bertha Starck!"

Of course I was a whole lot more surprised than she was, really, but it was pretty awful to see the stiffness go out of a person who had held herself straight and rigid for so many years, and the grim lines of her face soften and to hear her voice breaking that way.

"I'd thought to bury that name," she said, "with those who carried it. The others did . . ."

"You can't bury a name, Mrs. Mack, that's part of the history of a big business. And if you wanted to keep it buried why did you send that bottle with Fred's ship model in it to be sold at the Festival—a bottle with 'Starck & Sons' blown into the glass?"

"I guess I did it to be mean!" she said. "Fred never intended they should have it. He was making it just to pleasure himself. When he died, I figured I might bother them a little doing that. Henry Willoughby, maybe, or James Herrod—make them turn in their beds one night as their folks made me turn for many a night in mine."

"Who founded the business? Your grandfather Starck?"

"Yes."

"And your sister and you were brought up well off?"

"As good as the Willoughby girls or James Herrod's sons! Maybe better. The money wasn't divided between two families then."

Her face was grim again and her voice had got back all its hardness.

"It was Grandfather Starck who built 'The Pines,' too. I spent my summers in the house those Herrods, for two generations, have been saying's theirs."

"It is theirs, Mrs. Mack!"

"By trickery! It wouldn't have been if my father hadn't let himself be taken in by old Mr. Willoughby. Oh, I can remember all the grand talk about two business heads being better than one and how it was a good thing, sometimes, for an old company to take in new blood. And maybe it is if you're smart alike the Willoughbys and get yourself incorporated right off. But my father wasn't smart. He let them talk him into making it a partnership. It wasn't a year before they had frozen him out."

I'd never heard her talk a tenth as much. It just came pouring out as though, now she'd started, she couldn't stop it.

"The Herrods were in on the deal—weren't they?" Mark said. "James Herrod's father?"

"In on it! I should say so! Standing by with the money all salted away to buy it up after old Mr. Willoughby drove it, high, wide, and handsome, into bankruptcy court. Willoughby money, too—part of it—as my father well knew. Only they'd fixed it up so smart he couldn't prove it."

"Your father died?"

"He didn't live the year. And my mother right after him. All they saved out of it was the furniture that's in this house. The only reason they left us that, I've figured, is because it wasn't the style any longer and they had no use for it."

"And your sister and you . . . ?"

"The county orphaned us out. Me with a family here in town and my sister on a farm over near Thornton. It was the Richmonds, owned it. Charlie's father was the youngest son."

"Then your sister died?"

"Yes. Fred and I took Charlie in. He was a bright boy—a good boy, always. He could have gone in with Fred and made living enough up here, but he wasn't content with that. I guess it was in his blood. Had to go down to the city and make something of himself!" She stopped suddenly. "Is he going to die?"

I knew what Dr. Carver had said, that he thought he'd pull Mr. Richmond through, and Mark must have remembered that I'd heard it, too, because he looked at me, quick and sharp and caught my eye.

"You can't be sure, Mrs. Mack—where poison is concerned."

"Poison! It was poison then?" She stopped and you could see that she was having a terrible struggle with herself.

"Maybe it's part my fault!" she finally said. "Maybe I should have told Charlie his mother was a Starck—and all it meant. Maybe if I had, he'd stayed away from that crowd and not met Edith Willoughby's sister that was engaged to James Herrod, and run away with her. And James wouldn't have married Henrietta and made her life what it's been. And Henrietta wouldn't have hated Charles Richmond's wife for being the woman her husband really wanted . . . and never got over wanting. . . . And Henrietta wouldn't have given her that glass . . ."

Mrs. Mack had been sitting there, twisting and twisting the ring around her finger and talking in a high, strained monotone. But she broke off suddenly as though she had realized that she'd said more than she'd intended.

"Henrietta Herrod," Mark said quietly, "handed Mrs. Richmond a glass the night she died?"

"Oh, Mr. Crosby, I never meant . . . it's more than I'm up to, to carry tales . . . but Charlie's daughter going that way, and then Fred, and now . . . if I'd spoken sooner maybe nothing would have happened to any of them . . ."

The way she sat up, straight, and with her chin firm, you could see she had made up her mind.

"I'm not saying Henrietta Herrod killed Charlie's daughter, and I'm not saying she had anything to do with the way Fred drowned. I'm not even saying she poisoned Charlie, that's something I don't know.

"What I do know is, that the night Charlie's wife fell overboard from Fred's boat, Henrietta Herrod had just brought her a glass of wine. She was sitting up on the boat's rail so she could see the fireworks better. Fred was close by, tending to something about the rigging. She took the glass from Mrs. Herrod and drank the wine and she went stiff all over—Fred saw her with his own eyes—and he said she lost her balance and gave sort of a scream and fell into the water and the glass was still in her hand."

"And nobody else saw it happen? Nobody else has known it all these years?"

Mrs. Mack's head was drooping. She looked tired and sad and terribly old.

"Nobody but me . . ."

Mark stood up. "I'm sorry, Mrs. Mack. But I'm glad you told me, and I think you will be too after a while. Even if I had to lie to you a little to get that secret out. Charlie Richmond will pull through—at least that's what Dr. Carver says.

"What you've told me is important—terribly important. It's important that Mrs. Herrod saw Mrs. Richmond fall, heard her cry out, before she went overboard. For me that's the last link in the chain."

She was crying, but without making any sound.

"Will you tell me one more thing?" Mark said gently. "And then I'll let you alone, in peace."

She looked up and I saw her face and I knew I hated Mrs. Herrod more than I'd ever hated anybody in my life before.

"What was the charm that Fred left at home?"

For a minute you could see she couldn't think what he was talking about and then a sorry sort of a smile lifted the corner of her mouth and her lips quivered.

"Oh, just an old pipe," she said, and the tears started again and ran down the furrows of her face. "He always had a fancy it kept him safe."

"Yes, I thought so," Mark said. "And I'm afraid maybe he was right. Once he'd openly lined up with Charlie

Richmond again—and knowing what he knew—it probably did keep him safe."

I didn't say a word—I couldn't—when I went out with
him and climbed into the Fiat. Not until we'd driven over
and were walking along the shore where Alicia had died
and he told me about how I had to help him catch the person who'd been doing it all by just sitting there, meek and
mild, like bait in a trap.

We went back home and I tried to eat a little because
Mother's eagle eye was on me and then at eight o'clock I
got dressed and went over to the Willoughbys', the way
Mark had told me to, and sat down in the big wing chair
in their living room, and shivered beside the fire.

24

It seemed to me I'd been sitting there for hours watching the door for Mark and just keeping on saying no to everybody and getting more and more scared until I thought I wouldn't be able to move anyway, even when Mark did give me the sign to go ahead.

The big grandfather's clock in the Willoughbys' hallway struck nine and then nine-thirty in the slow, solemn way it had, and just before ten Mr. Herrod came over to me and said:

"Come on, Kitty, the fireworks are starting in five minutes. We're going to watch them from the boat."

I looked up at him and smiled and started to say no and then Mrs. Herrod's voice boomed:

"James, if you insist on boarding the *Felicity* in all this wind . . . I'm going along."

Mr. Herrod just sort of shrugged and I said, "Oh, but please . . . don't bother . . . I'd rather not." And then I absolutely froze. Because Mark was standing in the doorway nodding at me and I stared at him and he slipped back out of sight and I managed to say, "All right, Mr. Herrod," and got up and he drew my arm through his, and Mrs. Herrod stepped to the other side of me and I went out through the doorway between them, into the dark.

All the way down across the lawn the old pines groaned and their needles whispered and hissed. I felt as though I were walking in one of those terrible nightmares where you can't wake up unless you scream and you try and try and not a sound will come out of your throat.

Our footsteps echoed along the planking of the dock, and I kept thinking of all the people I'd ever read about who had walked, knowing it, to their deaths, and I kept saying, "Mark . . . Mark . . . Mark . . ." over and over again way down inside me and telling myself that he knew what he was doing and everything would be all right.

The *Felicity* was absolutely dark except for her high riding light that made a plunging arc as she pitched in the trough of the rollers that were coming in. The Herrods didn't stop at sight of her, though, but went right on in that awful march, one on each side of me like jailers, and Mr. Herrod climbed on board and held out his hands and helped us both up and I was shaking so my teeth chattered and I could hardly hold onto the rail.

"Why, Kitty," he said, "you're cold, child. I'll go in the cabin and find something to put around you." And I remember I had to bite my lip to keep from crying out, "No! No! Don't leave me alone with her! I'm afraid! I'm afraid!"

Mr. Herrod said, "Look, my dear, they've sent the first one up." And I saw a rocket rise and break in a thousand stars and the stars lighted the water where the combers were coming in, all along the shore. He laughed and slipped his hands under my arms and lifted me onto the rail, like a little girl, and said, "There! You can see better from there." And Mrs. Herrod stood beside me, grim as death, her mouth closed in a narrow slit.

And Mark wasn't anywhere in the world and I was lost and alone and I thought, in another minute I'll faint, and when I do I'll fall overboard, into that pounding water, and I felt something small and smooth and cool in my hand and with what sense I had left I realized that it was a lighter and that Mr. Herrod had opened his big silver case and was offering me a cigarette.

"Here, Kitty. Take one, my dear. I'll just step inside and get something to put around you," and I saw Mark's head and shoulders in the cabin doorway and he crossed the deck in two huge steps and I felt his hand, warm and hard, on mine, and I heard his voice.

"M-m-mr. Herrod, if you p-p-please! K-k-kathie is not used to more than the n-n-normal amount of nicotine in what she smokes."

And then I saw the others—Dr. Carver and Steve Brownlow and Art Stewart coming slowly up the companionway onto the deck of the *Felicity*.

"Like one yourself, Herrod? Or one of Richmond's cigars? Fixed 'em up pretty for us—didn't you?—before we took Alicia's body home. Mr. Richmond still has a few of them—choice specimens, I tell you! Thought the box would go down with the three of us, didn't you? Too bad we slipped up like that. Richmond had plenty in his case, so they didn't get around to that box until they were nearly home. Fred and Mr. Richmond, that is. And you wouldn't even have picked Fred off if we hadn't been in such a hurry to get away that Fred didn't have time to go back to his house and get his pipe. Too bad for Fred, Richmond's generous—told Fred to help himself to the cigars. It looks as though he did, all right, from the new box, before he went up on deck to take that last look of his at the weather.

"And then, Richmond—well, when he bit the end off the first cigar he'd taken from that box, he was in Dr. Carver's office and we were close on your trail by that time, so it only made him pretty damned sick. Too bad Richmond'll get well, isn't it? First aid and smoker's tolerance worked against you there. Just can't count on how a hard smoker'll react to the stuff, or on his being in the close vicinity of water—or a rock—when that vertigo hits him.

"As for me—sorry as hell, Herrod, but I don't smoke. Never have. Pretty slipshod in your observation there or you'd have doctored the rye we had on board. Special treat for me! I guess Mrs. Herrod thought you had doctored it for all of us.

"She, stuck by you, though, Herrod. Has all along. Got hold of those keys of Alicia's you've been making so free with and boarded the *Lark* last night to destroy the evidence."

Mark's smile, when he looked at Mrs. Herrod wasn't unfriendly but it was sad.

"You see, I knew you'd been on board, Mrs. Herrod, and I had some idea, anyway, of what you were after. So I checked up on the *Lark's* liquor supply this morning and found you'd cleaned us out. As it happens, I don't think you had to worry about that.

"Herrod only poisoned liquor—or rather, wine—once. Didn't you, Herrod? A long time ago. . . . But lately you thought you'd worked out something better. You had, too. Something foolproof—adding nicotine to nicotine. Trouble is, you were having too much fun and you got careless. If you're subtle enough, Herrod, and unscrupulous and you're a natural-born hypocrite, you've got a pretty good chance of getting away with one murder. And if you wait twenty-five years—maybe even with two. But three, Herrod, and an attempted fourth and fifth . . . No—that gets too thick."

I'd slipped down off the rail onto the deck and I'd found a bench I could sit on and hold to and I sat there, horribly fascinated, watching Mr. Herrod. His lips had begun to quiver and his face was all crumpled like a baby's that's going to cry.

"Henrietta . . ." he whimpered. "Henrietta . . . don't let them say things like that. They're lying . . ."

"James . . ." I looked up at Mrs. Herrod and I saw her eyes narrowed and the drawn lines around her mouth. ". . . for twenty-five years, James, I have lived with you knowing that you poisoned Janice Richmond! And this summer when that . . . that girl people said was your daughter . . . I don't believe she was. I believe you started that story yourself to make people think she'd been more to you than you could ever make her be. And to get even with Charles Richmond. This summer when she died, I tell you, I knew you had killed her! I knew it as well as if I'd seen you do it with your own hands. Because twenty-five years ago I saw you pour something into the glass you filled with wine and handed me to give to Janice Richmond. Only I didn't know that it was poison until I saw her die.

"You killed the girl for the same reason that you killed her mother—because you were sick with envy and jealousy of other people's happiness. Because you're a poor, weak, spineless creature whose only power has been in watching other people suffer and knowing you were behind it all.

"Ever since then—ever since Alicia Richmond died—I've watched you. I didn't know how you had managed to kill that girl but I did know how you had killed her mother. So I've watched you, followed you, tried never to let you out of my sight. Never to let you get away with giving any living person a glass or a cup or a bite of food with your own hands. But you're slippery, James—I couldn't always keep you in sight. I didn't see you board that boat—the Richmonds'—before it sailed, but I saw you leave it, and I knew that somehow—somewhere—you had a key to it. I went through everything you had, looking, until I found those keys.

"What did you do, James Herrod—find her purse where Helen Willoughby had put it that night on the beach? Did you hunt for it in all the baskets while the rest of us were trying to bring order out of the confusion of her murder?"

Mr. Herrod made a funny, choking sound in his throat, but she didn't pay any attention to him. She went right on.

"Never mind! It doesn't matter . . . I only want you to know, James, that I've watched you, not to save your miserable skin but to protect my family—your family—to save our good name. Well, I couldn't save it . . . it's gone now . . . and I'm through . . . I don't care what happens . . ."

She broke into a sobbing that was so awful, I suppose, because she hadn't let herself break down and cry for years. It seemed terribly strange to me to be doing it, but I reached out and took Mrs. Herrod's hand and sat there holding it hard, between mine.

"Henrietta . . . I didn't, I tell you . . . They're lying . . . It's something you've imagined . . . something they've made up! They can't prove it!"

"Dr. Carver," Mark said, "you have the pen?"

Dr. Carver reached in an inside pocket and took it out and it was the one I'd picked up at Willoughbys' and brought to Mark, only now it had the cap on it.

"Dr. Carver, are you ready to testify that the well of this pen—the rubber sack that usually contains ink—was filled with nicotine? The pure, concentrated alkaloid?"

"Certainly, Crosby. I told you that."

"And are you ready to testify, also, that while the cigars which Mr. Richmond habitually smokes contain approximately 1.28% nicotine, by weight, the cigar from which he bit the tip before he was taken so seriously ill in your office, contained 8.721%?"

"I gave you the figures, Crosby."

"Yes, doctor. Thank you.

"Mr. Herrod, I'm afraid your game is, up. This is your pen. Here are your initials, engraved on the gold band around the cap. Willoughby saw you—came on you suddenly in his tool shed and startled you so that you dropped it—didn't he?—when you were filling it from the bottle of nicotine he uses in dilute solution for spraying plants? When you were filling it and fixing up a few last ciga- rettes? Was one of them for Willoughby? Probably. At any rate he thought so.

"It must have put you out—dropping your pen that way and knowing Willoughby was bound to find it. Then Willoughby taking sick leave tonight and not showing up so that you could offer him a smoke! And on top of that seeing the pen in the front of Kathie's blouse this after- noon and meeting her coming from Willoughby's shed again a little later. Don't think I don't understand, Her- rod. Hard on your nerves, I know. Of course you had to get rid of Kathie, didn't you?

"Because she had foundry your pen—*your* pen, Herrod, filled with the nicotine that had poisoned four people. The nicotine that you dropped into the cigarette you just offered her. It doesn't take much, especially for a woman, and then, inhaling . . . well, you're bound to absorb about eight times as much as you do if you don't inhale.

"Only death we can try you for is Alicia's, of course, because her body is the only corpus delicti your unique schemes for self-disposal left us. It's not going to be much trouble, though, to convince a jury that that pen of yours was the weapon with which you killed her. The instrument you used to put nicotine into the cigarette you gave her. Oh, no—we haven't the cigarette. That washed out to sea. But tied up with Richmond's cigars and a few other little odds and ends, like the contents of your pen—well . . . it's circumstantial, but men have been hanged on less . . ."

I was watching Mark all the time he was talking, so I didn't see it happen when Mr. Herrod swung himself up onto the rail and snapped open his silver case, but I saw the flare of the match he struck, and I saw the cigarette be- tween his lips and I saw his eyes, terribly afraid, and I heard him cry out in that dreadful way and I saw him fall . . .

And there wasn't anything there any more in the dark except the fireworks that had kept going up all the time— rockets and Roman candles falling in showers of colored stars—and there wasn't any sound except the break of the waves against the pilings and the boat, and the voices of people, laughing and calling to each other on shore, very far away, and then Mrs. Herrod's voice that didn't sound like hers at all, pleading . . .

"Drowned . . . can't you say he was drowned . . . does anyone need to know . . . ?"

And I didn't know anything at all except that Mark's arms were around me, keeping me safe, and that the soft, rough leather of his jacket was against my face, and that he was sheltering me close from the wind and the fine, cold rain that had begun to beat in from the east.

About the Author

Eleanor Atkinson was born in July 1899 in Hinsdale, Illinois. Eleanor was the daughter of journalists and authors Francis Blake Atkinson and Eleanor Stackhouse Atkinson (most famed for the 1912 novel *Greyfriars Bobby*). Eleanor's sister, as Dorothy Blake, wrote magazine pieces and family novels *(The Diary of a Suburban Housewife* and *It's All in the Family)*. Eleanor married advertising copywriter George Wallace Cox in 1922, and had two children, Eleanor and Wallace (but soon divorced after her son was born). Her son was actor Wally Cox (1924-1973). Wally noted in one interview that his mother was nomadic, traveling around the country, and that he attended nine schools in twelve years. She wrote for a Chicago newspaper for ten years. As a journalist for a Detroit newspaper during prohibition, Eleanor wrote a feature story recounting her adventure first riding with a rum runner smuggling alcohol from Canada to Ohio, then joining the Coast Guard as they chased the smuggler. During the 1930s, she remarried, to Benson K. Pratt. Eleanor and her family lived in Omena, Michigan; the Omena-Northport area inspired the setting for *Death Down East*. Eleanor wrote two mysteries as well as regional novels (such as *Seed Time and Harvest*). Eleanor died in West Nyack, New York, January 14, 1952.

COACHWHIP PUBLICATIONS
ALSO AVAILABLE

COACHWHIPBOOKS.COM (PRINT)
COACHWHIP.COM (EPUB)

COACHWHIP PUBLICATIONS
ALSO AVAILABLE

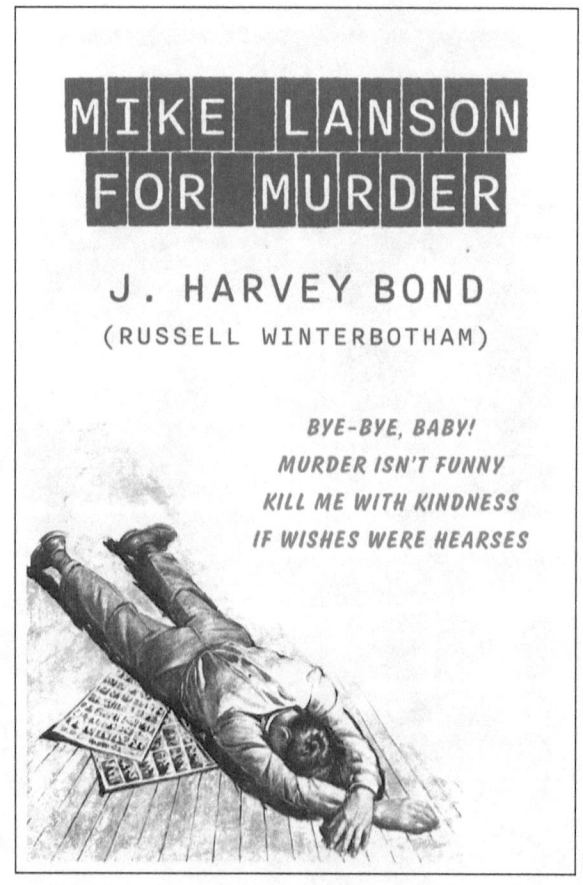

MIKE LANSON FOR MURDER

J. HARVEY BOND

(RUSSELL WINTERBOTHAM)

BYE-BYE, BABY!
MURDER ISN'T FUNNY
KILL ME WITH KINDNESS
IF WISHES WERE HEARSES

COACHWHIP PUBLICATIONS
ALSO AVAILABLE

A SULTAN'S HAREM MYSTERY

Drink the Green Water
The Milkmaid's Millions

HUGH AUSTIN

COACHWHIPBOOKS.COM (PRINT)
COACHWHIP.COM (EPUB)

Death Has
Seven Faces

HUGH AUSTIN

DEATH
ON THE CAMPUS
ADDISON
SIMMONS